VAMPIRE LIBRARIAN

THE SHADOW ORDER: VAMPIRE BOOK ONE

KRISTIN KOVA

☾

Want an email when new books release - and two freebies?

Sign up for my newsletter: https://sendfox.com/kristinkova

Or join me on Facebook: https://www.facebook.com/kristinkovaauthor

☾

Cover by Open World Cover Design

 Created with Vellum

No harm ever came from reading a book...

THE MUMMY (1999)

KRISTIN KOVA

VAMPIRE
LIBRARIAN

THE SHADOW ORDER: VAMPIRE 1

ONE

THE CLIENT WAS TWENTY MINUTES LATE.

I shifted in my chair in the west archives of the Witching Library, peering at the door to the main library chamber. No one marched through it in a power suit or designer label coat; everything was quiet and still except for the tapping of rain on the tall windows to my right and pages rustling next door.

Where the hell was he? He was supposed to be here at six to collect the Codex of Fiends, the massive, dusty tome sat on the table in front of me. I'd had to unlock a magically sealed glass cabinet to access this book, twenty feet up an ancient wooden ladder that threatened to drop me to the floor in a plume of tartan, wool, and bright red hair. He'd better not ghost me.

I could have been at home right now, curled up in front of the fire with Aunt Jubilee's army of pets instead of shivering in the draughty archive waiting for someone almost certainly rich and entitled to collect his book.

I loved every inch of this place, though. The library had become a second home and a more than welcome distraction from everything that went on with my family six months ago. It was a chance to prove I wasn't like Leona, my sister—to my mum , to my aunt, and to myself.

"Come on," I muttered, glancing at the clock on the aged brick wall, stone claws of gargoyles holding it to the wall. Not real gargoyles, obviously—those were way bigger than a two-foot clock, and much more brooding.

Even if the Witching Library was freezing cold, I never stopped feeling grateful for being able to come to a hallowed, ancient space every day—and to get paid for it.

History was shelved all around me, and even the newest books had their stories to tell—scratches from careless owners, pages loosened by overzealous readers, warped circles on pages where they'd moved people to tears. I loved finding those little marks, collected them like clues to a mystery.

The absent client's book—the Codex of Fiends—was no different. It might have been one of the oldest, most powerful books in the archive, but it had its own dents and tears and dog-eared pages. It also happened to contain deadly rituals, fatal spells, and an encyclopaedia of demons.

Not my kinda read, but to each their own. I'd just finished a romance about a witch and a werewolf, but I fancied something darker, with intrigue and mystery, for my next obsession. Maybe the client would show up in the next few minutes, and I'd have time to go up to the fiction section on the library's fourth mezzanine.

"Where are you?" I huffed, turning in my chair to glance at the doorway. Again.

It was always cold in this part of the library, but I shuddered at a rush of frigid air, wrapping my tartan cardigan tighter around myself. It had cats knitted into the fabric, a tiny army of them guarding the big patch pockets

I stored fun-size packets of Haribo and random gemstones in.

Maybe the client had gotten lost.

Or maybe he'd been attacked on the way here. There'd been strange reports coming from the east end of London where my best friend Ruby lived. The attacks involved all three orders of supernaturals—Shadow, Light, *and* Beast—which never happened.

Not quite murders, people had been found drained of blood and vital fluids until they were empty shells of themselves. The attacks practically screamed *vampire*, but the Shadow Order refused to claim the crimes because of a single anomaly: the victims were left alive.

Any vampire attacker would drain someone to death, which made these attacks ... weird. The council *hated* weirdness.

Everyone was freaked out, myself included. I lived in the opposite direction, but that didn't make living and working in a city rife with attacks any easier. A chill skated down my spine, and I groaned at the clock on the wall, every tick mocking me. I tried not to think of the roaring fire, thick blanket, and pack of cats and huskies waiting at home.

After another few minutes, I lifted the codex into my arms and went in search of my lost client, all patience fizzling into nothing.

"The least you could do was call and cancel," I muttered, my annoyed footsteps echoing off the high stone ceilings.

The main room of the library was ten times bigger than the section I worked in, and it was full of towering book-shelves from end to end, with a row of desks cutting down the middle where people usually sat to read. The chairs were all empty tonight. The rustle of pages I'd thought had come from people studying was actually because the main door had been left wide open.

With a frown, I set off to shut it. My boss Ursula would throw a hissy fit when she found out someone had left the door open, wind driving the rain inside.

I only made it two steps before hairs rose on the back of my neck, and my vision split into twenty shards of rainbow colours—twenty glimpses of the future. My gift as a seer manifested at odd times, but for it to show now when the empty room already had me nervous...

I had a bad feeling about this.

A pale wrist with a heavy, expensive watch filled one bright shard. Blood spilled across a polished floor in another. Empty eyes stared at me from yet another shard. And in the biggest, most insistent vision, shadows crept across the foyer seeking, searching. Hungry.

I jolted out of the vision with a gasp, my heart pounding. Shit. Someone was hurt, or about to be. And worse, I couldn't shake the certainty that they were here somewhere in the library. And I was in danger.

Without a second thought, I turned and fled back into the archives, my shoes squeaking on the parquet floor and my breathing suddenly too loud.

My arms began to shake around the codex when I heard the whoosh of fast-moving fabric, footsteps barely meeting the floor but loud enough for me to pick them up as I fled. I pressed a cry between my lips, seeing the future in my fractured vision: a dead body, a pool of blood, and hungry darkness that wanted to devour me.

That *would* devour me.

That was my client I saw dead on the ground, not an indistinct blur of something that *might* happen but a crystal clear scene of something that already *had*.

He'd been murdered, and his killer was still in the library.

When I'd said I wanted a story full of intrigue and mystery, I meant to *read* it, not be the main fucking character.

I could barely breathe as I flung myself around the corner of a bookshelf in the archives, hiding in the gloom between the stacks and listening intently. My panicked breaths were too loud, my heartbeat too harsh, especially if the killer was a supernatural with advanced hearing.

Was this the person who'd attacked supernaturals in the east end?

I shook my head. That didn't matter; I had to get out of here, and I couldn't afford to think about anything else.

There was a window big enough for me to fit through, but it was high enough that I'd need a ladder. I carefully backed down the dim aisle and scanned the shelves until I found the tall, rolling ladder. The chances of me moving it without being heard were slim to none, but I had to do *something*.

I held the codex to my chest with one arm—at this point it was my safety blanket—and grabbed the ladder with my free hand, my breath stuttering at the deep rumble as it moved on its track. My knees were so weak they threatened to drop me onto the floor.

All I had to do was move the ladder close to the wall, and I could climb it and scramble out the window. I'd figure out how to get down the other side later, when I wasn't in the same building as a murderer.

Wait—the client was dead. My vision confirmed it in another flash of gleaming shards. He'd bled out on the floor.

But the east end attacker left their victims *alive*. What the hell was going on here? Was this just an enemy of the client's catching up to him? The library served important, influential people all the time; maybe it had nothing to do with the attacks. I couldn't let panic cloud my judgement.

"Found it," a deeply amused voice crowed, and I jumped so hard I let go of the ladder. It clattered against the bookcase, the noise making me breathless.

My heart jumped into my throat, and I stumbled back on feet I could barely feel, not stopping until my back met the solid wall with a thump. Someone had killed my client, and now they were here to kill me.

Fight or flight kicked in hard, even as panicked tears stung my eyes.

"Back off! I'm armed," I warned weakly, watching an indistinct shadow move through the stacks toward me.

I wasn't armed, but he didn't need to know that. My vision split and flashed, and I scanned the technicolour visions for an escape.

There were no ways out. Not a single one.

My heart drummed harder, a panicked prey animal frantically searching for a way to safety.

But in one of my shards, I saw something that made me sick with terror. He was a vampire—faster, stronger, and superior in every way to a seer like me. I might have been fit from hauling books every day, but I wasn't fit enough to outrun a *vampire*.

The vampire snorted, suddenly inches in front of me. I flinched so hard my head smacked the stone wall, pain exploding through my skull and dragging a whimper up my throat. Shit. Oh fuck, I was going to die. I hadn't even blinked, and he was right in my face.

He was beautiful, truly and flawlessly, but that was as much a weapon crafted to kill as his fangs and speed.

Hunger shone through red eyes, and I saw death, both in his stare and in my visions.

"I have holy water," I lied, flinching as the rain drummed harder on the windows outside, a mocking rattle like an audience's laughter. My arms shook around the codex, and I held it tighter, my life raft in a killer storm.

I was going to die here, and I couldn't see a way out no matter how frantically I searched my futures.

The vampire snorted at my weak warning, his mouth in a cruel smile. He was the worst kind of person—not just someone who hurt others out of necessity, but one who enjoyed it.

"I doubt you even have spring water. Give me the book."

I blinked, stunned for a long, sticky second before the vampire shook my shoulders with bruising hands, my brain bouncing around inside my skull until I was disoriented and dumb.

"*Let go,*" he demanded, slashing sharp fingernails through my cardigan and into my shoulders.

My rattled brain couldn't connect the dots. All I could do was stare at the spots dancing around my vision—pure dizziness this time, not clairvoyance—and slur an ill-advised, "*You* let go."

Off balance and dizzy with fear, I toppled forward. By pure chance, the momentum slammed my torso into the vampire's chest with a brutal smack. I was nowhere near strong enough to dislodge him with brute force, but the surprise caught him off guard long enough for one of his hands to slip off my shoulder.

The only thought in my head was *oh, gods, I'm going to die here*.

"Let go!"

I couldn't breathe, especially as sharp claws gouged my

forearm, cutting a deep scratch through wool and flesh before I could even blink.

I cried out as all my senses were replaced by the sharp burn of pain and the acidic taste of copper on my tongue. *Fuck*, it hurt. I bit the inside of my lip, my eyes stinging as the pain intensified even more.

I could barely see, but that didn't stop me wrenching away and taking off down the aisle when the vampire hissed, distracted by my blood. I stumbled as fast as my jelly legs would carry me—away from the ladder, the window, and salvation. I'd lost all logic; all I had were flight instincts now, my hindbrain screaming like a banshee sensing death.

My fingers were still locked around the codex like the gnarled roots of a tree, and as I scrambled down the aisle towards the heart of the circular room, it hit me.

He wanted this book. That was why the client was dead, and why the vampire hadn't killed me on sight: he didn't want to risk damaging the codex. Even a drop of blood on the cover could affect something as old and powerful as this in ways no one could ever predict.

But what the hell did a vampire want with an encyclopaedia of demons?

And why scratch me? Why make me bleed? Unless he hadn't meant to...

The shelves and desks of the archive blurred as I ran as fast as I could, air sawing out of my lungs like a bellows. I flinched at my own footsteps as they rebounded off the high ceilings, the vampire's pursuit silent and impossible to predict.

The scratch on my arm burned like I'd spilled hot oil on it; I whimpered with every breath.

I was a librarian, for fuck's sake! I wasn't designed for fighting vampires and running for my life.

I made it to the big arched door at the edge of the room before air whooshed behind me and a hand closed around my throat.

"No!" I recoiled hard, tears welling in my eyes as the fight for my life became terrifyingly, inescapably real. Bruising, icy fingers pressed on my windpipe and I cried at the flash of yet more pain.

The codex fell from my arms, my body shaking too hard to hold onto it, and a shadow stepped in front of me from the depths of the main chamber.

I was frozen, held still by the fingers crushing my throat as the shadow bent in an elegant arch to retrieve it from the floor, the air perfumed with honey and my own blood.

"Thank you so much," the newcomer said in a warm, inviting voice. When he straightened, I swallowed hard. He was a vampire, too, with ice-pale skin and sculpted cheekbones, his lips arranged in a pleasant smile—hiding deadly fangs. He was even more beautiful than the other man, which meant he was far more dangerous.

Their beauty was directly proportionate to how easily they could kill.

"What's your name?" he asked in a friendly voice, peering at my face as I trembled in his friend's—henchman's—arms.

"Keaton," he tsked. "How's the lady supposed to talk with your ham hands cutting off her air supply?"

"Don't know why you insist on talking to 'em," the man choking me—Keaton, apparently—muttered, loosening his icy grip on my neck.

I dragged in frantic gulps of air, my eyes wide with terror. I'd never been so close to an apex predator before. The closest I'd come to danger was when a werewolf growled at me in protest of his library fees when I was a junior librarian, and *he'd* never actually touched me.

This ... I wanted to run, but I was frozen, shaking, petrified to the spot. I wanted to scream, but my voice refused to form. All I could do was gasp through the pain.

"Your name, sweet thing," the charming vampire repeated, not a single strand on his glossy blond head moving out of place as he tilted it to look at me. My heart jolted at the eye contact, and I glanced swiftly away.

Everyone knew the rules about vampires:

Never go anywhere alone with one.

Never look them in the eyes.

And never, *ever* let them bite or scratch you.

I shook my head, not sure if I was stupid or brave to keep my name to myself. But I didn't know what kind of psychopaths they were—the kind to only play with me, or to hunt down my whole family. There were as many horror stories in the news as there were supernaturals in the world, and I couldn't risk my family like that.

But what they'd do to me... My stomach rocked, bile splashing up my throat. Oh, fuck, I was dead.

The charming vampire laughed, even that sound warm and soft, coaxing me to trust him, to look up, to meet his eyes. One second of eye contact, and he'd compel me.

What would he compel me to do? I'd rather die than be chained to him as a food source. And that was my *best* case scenario.

"Shall we take hers, too?" Keaton asked, his cool breath fanning over the shell of my ear and making me tremble harder. The scratch on my arm intensified, painful and scalding.

Move, I screamed at myself. *Run! Fight them! Do some-*

thing other than stand here like a fucking idiot, waiting for death.

"No," the other vampire replied.

I jumped as cold fingers skimmed my chin and tilted my face up. I didn't close my eyes fast enough; he ensnared me in his gaze and I swayed forward with a broken gasp.

"He won't like this one," he went on, talking to Keaton but staring deep into my eyes.

It was like meeting a god's eyes—terrifying and endless, full of power and terrible beauty. In his blue eyes, I saw his descent to hell, and I knew he'd drag me down with him.

"Stop," I breathed, all I could manage—a tiny, wisp of a word. I barely heard it, but I had no doubt they both did.

"Thank you for the book," he said with a lovely smile, his fingers trailing the shape of my cheek while his other hand held the codex.

I couldn't even flinch, my body was so entirely locked. The towering library faded around me, its tall, arched windows and impressive stacks turning to pure, inky blackness. The scent of old paper and ink was replaced by honey and blood, the ground non-existent beneath my feet. Even Keaton's hand around my throat and his scratch on my arm slid away, every sense consumed by the vampire in front of me.

As if he'd wordlessly compelled me to see only him.

"On the off chance you survive, forget Keaton," he purred, his stare keeping me captive. "Forget the codex. But remember me."

Everything in my body went as tense as a bowstring when he peeled Keaton's hand from my throat and slammed his own palm into my chest hard enough to fracture my ribs.

His impossible strength propelled me across the room,

over the tables and chairs. Air sliced past me, whipping my hair into my face, disorienting and fast. I was … flying?

Helpless and dazed, I crashed into the furthest bookshelf. As the two vampires laughed under their breath, I felt my body break.

TWO

I SCREAMED AS I FLEW THROUGH THE AIR. MY HEAD slammed into a heavy wooden shelf, rattling me so hard I got whiplash and sending an explosion of pain through my skull. The spines of leather books bit into my neck as I crashed to the ground, every part of me blazing with agony and a hazy sort of shock as I splayed there.

What...?

I shook my head, hissing at a spike of dizziness, trying to stitch my thoughts together.

How did I get here? I'd fallen...? It didn't seem right, but that was the only plausible explanation.

The shelf behind me wobbled dangerously, an ominous groan of wood making me flinch. My breath caught as the shelf tipped, air rushing above my head as it toppled.

Only pure instinct and adrenaline allowed me to drag my wrecked body across the floor, my teeth gritted against the pain. Sweet pricked the back of my neck as I dug my fingernails into the wooden slats of the floorboards and hauled myself inch by inch, barely able to hear my panting breaths over the groan and howl of bookshelves shifting.

"Help," I rasped, lifting my head. But I was alone.

There'd been a man...

A sob caught in my throat, confusion and panic over-whelming my emotions, but I pushed the rubber soles of my shoes against the floorboards and used the grip to propel myself forward. Tears stinging my eyes, I fell against a chair in the middle of the room with heaving breaths, my head spinning as I stared at the bookcase I'd crawled away from.

As if in slow motion, the massive bookcase lost its battle with gravity and tilted too far forward, box files and books spilling out with solid thumps on the floor. I could barely breathe as I watched it, my heart crashing against my ribs and cold spreading down my spine.

All that history, all those valuable books...

I couldn't take my eyes off the falling bookcase as it smacked into the one beside it, sending that one toppling, too.

"Oh gods," I whispered, my blurry eyes fixed on the bookshelves as they fell, one by one, in a destructive domino effect that left me sitting in the middle of chaos.

How? *How* had I fallen into the bookcase hard enough to knock it over? Each one was carved from a single block of wood, and weighed ten times more than me. It didn't make sense, but I was too dizzy and pained to figure it out.

I tentatively touched my ribs, and hissed at a pulse of sharp, slicing pain. Bruised, if not broken.

The ladder ... I must have fallen off it. But how did I hurt my arm? I had a blazing, throbbing scratch down my forearm, and even a blurry glance at it made me wince. It was a mess of red skin and blood. Did I cut myself when I was up the ladder, getting the—

Getting the what?

I rubbed the headache forming between my eyebrows

and groaned, dragging myself to my feet. A flash of pain made me gasp, and I slumped into the table, curling my hands into fists as I waited for it to pass.

I had to do something about the scratch on my arm, or it was going to get infected. Or maybe it already was, and that was why I felt clammy and dizzy. I couldn't even feel the chill of the archives anymore; my body was too hot.

Gritting my teeth, I carefully peeled up the sleeve of my tartan cardigan so I could see the wound properly. There was a deep gouge up the centre of my forearm, the cut spiderwebbed with dark red at the edges. Definitely infected.

"I'm fucked," I gasped, staring at the mess of my arm and breathing jaggedly, each inhale so painful against my bruised ribs that tears stung my eyes.

I must have sliced my arm on one of the cabinets holding the library's ancient, valuable books. I needed to go to the hospital before I lost my damn arm, but I'd be lucky if I even made it there with how dizzy I was.

Why hadn't anyone run in from the main room to investigate the sound of the shelves crashing?

And where had that man gone? I remembered a vague impression of red eyes and sleek blond hair, an intense stare that made my heart catch—and not in a good way. He could be a psychopath for all I knew.

Had he told me his name? Why had he even been here? I didn't remember him checking out a book, but maybe I hadn't been paying attention. It was getting late; I was tired. That probably explained my murky memory; after a good night's sleep, things would come back to me.

I expelled a hard sigh and pushed shakily off the desk, staring at the mess of broken wood and trashed books around me. I was going to get fired for this. And then what would I be? A jobless twenty-seven year old, living with her mum and aunt, with nothing to show for her life except a string of broken relationships, a master's degree in arcane history, and a bedroom full of fairy lights and paintings in various states of completion.

I'd be just like Leona, a disappointment. Maybe they wouldn't even mention me anymore, like they didn't talk about my sister. The thought made me flinch. I had to find a way to fix this. I *couldn't* turn out like Leona.

Maybe Ursula would be lenient if I came in tomorrow in crutches, looking pitiful. Or if I phoned her from the hospital to explain what had happened. If there was ever a silver lining to having to see a nurse, looking pathetic enough to keep my job was it.

With painful steps, I dragged myself across the page-strewn floor to the main room. But I froze on the edge of the cavernous space, shades of memories trying and failing to form. Was the room colder here, or was that just my paranoia?

I brushed the fingers of my good arm over my throat, not sure why it was so tender to the touch. It must have been when I fell into the bookcase and sent it toppling. Fuck, *everything* on my body hurt.

There was a first-aid kit in Ursula's office, but I knew that wouldn't be enough to fix me up. I had to go to the hospital, no matter how reluctant I was. There was something about the smell of the place that made me feel small and afraid, a persistent sense of loss and grief I'd been too young to understand when Dad died.

"Hello?" I called into the empty room, taking slow, painstaking steps across the shining floor. I grabbed one of the study tables for support as pain shot up my side, fracturing out from my ribs. "Has everyone gone home? Is there anyone still here?"

I didn't like how small and afraid my voice came out.

The library was normally open twenty-four hours to accommodate nocturnal species, and there was *always* a librarian on hand. Had there been an earthquake or fire, and I'd missed it? My memory was spotty and dark when I reached for it. The last thing I could clearly remember was saying bye to my best friend Ruby when her shift ended, my client ghosting me, and then ... there'd been a man? Maybe?

My head hurt trying to remember, so I left it be.

I took another few steps, a muscle in my jaw fluttering as I gritted my teeth against the pain. I felt like I'd lost a fight with a freight train and scraped my shattered bones up off the rail tracks. I was never using a ladder again in my whole life.

I paused, leaning against a desk to get my phone from the pocket in my cardigan where it lived, on silent, while I worked—and I swore colourfully at the cracked screen. Great, now I had to find the money to get it replaced. With the possibility of being fired hanging over my head. Tonight was just getting better and better.

I held my breath as I punched the home button, even my fingertips screaming with pain and the cut on my forearm blazing like a bonfire under my skin. I couldn't hold back my cry of relief when the screen lit up, fractured and smashed, but still working.

"Thank you," I murmured to whatever god was watching over me. "Thank you."

My throat was hoarse, too, like I'd been screaming. Ugh, I wished I could remember what I'd done to make the book-shelf fall. Maybe there really had been an earthquake.

My finger hovered over Mum's name in my phone book,

but she'd fly into a state of panic if I said a bookcase had fallen on top of me. Or *I'd* fallen on a bookcase. Or whatever had actually happened. It made no sense, but trying to remember sent a spike of agony through my head. I hissed, rubbing at my temples.

The guttural hiss gave me pause, and my hand froze on my forehead. My voice was deeper, stranger.

I couldn't put it off anymore; I needed to get to the hospital *now*. Which meant phoning 666 for supernatural emergency services, not Mum.

My finger hovered over the 6 button, but fire flashed up my arm, strong enough to make me gasp. I stared at the scratch on my forearm, genuinely expecting to see flames. Okay, so there was absolutely no doubt it was infected. Fuck.

What was I supposed to do? What if an ambulance arrived too late?

Another surge of stabbing heat radiated from the cut and my phone dropped from my hand as my fingers flexed without my permission. I fell back against the desk, panting hard, my head spinning. I needed to get my phone, make the call, and wait for the paramedics—but I could barely hang on to the table and stay upright.

I wanted my mum.

Somewhere outside, a siren blared, but it was too far away to help me. A cat's throaty meow of warning reached me, too, and a couple arguing over the cost of Christmas presents.

I shook my head, breathing harder, faster. I drew breath to shout for help, but it cut out with the next wave of hot agony. I couldn't see the library anymore, just a smear of darkness and light. My knees weakened. The ground rushed at me, my hands barely catching me before my teeth met the floor.

The fire spread up my arm to my shoulder and chest, and I knew, deep down, an ambulance would get here too late to save me. Something was happening, infection spreading deeper, reaching my heart, and all I could do was curl my hands into fists and struggle to breathe.

I could smell my own blood, and the coppery scent of ... someone else's blood? Why was there someone else's blood in the library? Not to mention the ash and fire scent of a vampire threaded among the brittle paper and ink smell of books and waxy floor polish.

Something was wrong with me.

I needed that blond-haired man to come back; I could beg him for help. He might know CPR, might have been a nurse or doctor if I was lucky enough.

But no footsteps reached my throbbing ears, only my own voice as I screamed through gritted teeth—and then loudly, unrestrained. The howl ripped up my throat as fire exploded into every part of me, blotting out the chill of the library and the feel of the floor under me.

I fell onto my side, tears on my face, and knew I was dying. I saw it with my fractured sight: gravestones and coffins and pale, pale skin where it had once been warm honey.

I saw my heart stop, my breathing grow still, and I saw myself from above as I fell onto my back and splayed there, dead.

Rainbows splintered and slashed across my vision like shards of broken glass, and in them I saw ... I saw my eyes open again, crimson red. I saw myself lift my hands and stare at the sharp claws on the tips of my fingers, saw myself poke sharp teeth with my tongue and sit up with a look of pure panic on my face, the movement far, *far* too fast to be normal.

To be *living*.

The burning, the scratch, the man I could barely remember ... it all made sense.

I wasn't dying. I was becoming a vampire.

THREE

I LEFT THE DOOR TO THE WITCHING LIBRARY's security room open behind myself as I sped inside, my body moving scarily fast. I slammed into the chair set up in front of a dozen screens, my head reeling at my speed. I felt like a newborn giraffe, unwieldy and disconnected from my limbs.

When I snapped out of the shock, I hunted down the tapes of tonight's recording and broke them in two, erasing the digital backup for good measure. I couldn't let *anyone* see what had happened to me, what I'd become.

I was a seer from the Light Order. Unremarkable, ordinary, and plain. I wasn't ... I wasn't a vampire. I couldn't be. It wouldn't matter if I was still a seer, I'd be thrown in with every other Shadow Order creature—dark maji, reapers, necromancers, and demons. I was nothing like a demon.

My transition had happened exactly as I saw it in my vision: my heart had stopped and everything went black and empty, a pit of deathless nothing, but then I woke with a ragged breath in a new, stranger, stronger body, with senses that overwhelmed me until I wanted to scream.

I could still hear the couple arguing about money

several streets away. A TV was playing in the flat above the laundrette across the road, and the slouchy footsteps of someone on their way home after a tiring day at work reached my ears. I shouldn't have been able to hear *any* of those things, but they stabbed at my senses like annoying gnats, stealing my concentration as I erased the last clip of tonight's security footage.

"How the hell did this happen?" I rasped, my eyes stinging and tears forming—blood tears, I'd found when I burst into terrified sobs when the truth settled in after long minutes of just sitting there in the main room, alive and strong and superior in every way to my feeble seer form. I cried *blood* now.

I didn't want to think about what else I did with blood; I couldn't even entertain the idea.

The man in my blurry memory had scratched me. He had to have. But why? Why change a random archivist who had no connections he could take advantage of, no valuable family heirlooms, no secret fortune.

Vampires were vain and power hungry; they turned people who benefitted them, or at least those who made other vampires envious of them. I wasn't a stunning beauty other people would be jealous of; I was plain, but pretty enough. I wasn't an incredible singer, or an actress who turned heads, or a dancer who brought people to tears.

I was a librarian, and no matter how good I was at my job, I wasn't going to be the envy of all of London's supernatural populace any time soon. Unless they wanted a 1500s book of shadows with original annotations and scorch marks where it had been rescued from a witch trials, I didn't have a skill that would impress. I was an okay artist, but I had a long way to go before anyone was awed by my work. I certainly couldn't imagine a vampire turning me because of it.

Was it accidental? I reached for my memory, but hissed in pain at the slice of pain. Transitioning hadn't unlocked that part of my brain, that was for sure.

Fuck. I stared at the mess of ruined tapes, realising too late that the answers laid there. And I'd destroyed them in a rush of panic to preserve my old life.

I poked my sharp fangs with my tongue, unable to leave them alone—that undeniable proof of my new species. I could have written off everything else—even my death and rebirth could be a mere delusion caused by the infection of the cut on my arm.

But the cut had healed, my heart no longer thumped inside my chest, and I was ... cold. Inside and out.

Colder still when I looked at the wrecked surveillance tapes.

My heart ached when I thought of the fire blazing at home, of the dogs I could snuggle up with. There was no point going to a hospital anymore; they could do nothing for me.

So ... home then?

I swallowed, testing my hunger—or thirst. I didn't *feel* thirsty, but I wasn't sure how that would even feel. Any story I'd ever read about vampires said their hunger was ferocious and impossible to ignore. I'd have known if I was hungry, right?

I exhaled a sigh, the sound smoother and more beautiful than any I'd made before, and scrunched up my face when I fished my phone from my cardigan pocket—far too fast. Out of control.

My phone dropped to the floor, and yet more cracks

spread across its surface. Shame vampire venom didn't work on technology.

"I'd like to report a robbery," I practised, grabbing my phone from the floor. I winced, my words rushing out too fast. I needed to slow down; everything was on super speed. I took a tight breath and repeated, "I'd like to report a robbery."

Better, but I sounded breathless and panicked. I needed to be calm when I made the call, so no one would suspect me. I'd say I returned to the library because ... because I'd forgotten my phone, and then found the archives trashed.

I dragged a slow breath of air into my lungs, thrown off balance by the stillness of my heart. Was the room freezing cold, or was that just me?

"You can do this. You got this, Karina," I whispered to myself, crossing the second floor to the mezzanine that overlooked the main chamber where I'd transitioned. My thoughts again returned to the shadowy man I could almost remember, a mystery I kept prodding as often as I poked my new teeth with my tongue.

I was still in shock. When the truth really, finally settled in that there was no way back, that I was stuck this way, I'd break down. I wanted to be home when that happened, safe within the four walls I knew and trusted. Not in the same building where I was turned. Attacked? I wished I could remember.

Or maybe my memory was being kind by blotting it out. Maybe it was too traumatic to remember.

I took a deep breath and dialled 666, stumbling through an explanation: I was at the Witching Library and we'd been robbed. I didn't leave a name and I withheld my number, but at least someone knew about the crime. With any luck, they'd find the man who'd turned me. My ... my sire.

I shuddered to think about it, and then I shook myself.

"Enough," I hissed in that guttural voice, looking down at the library. Pages were scattered across the floor and an eerie stillness hung over everything where there was usually bustling activity. Had the vampire who turned me sent everyone away with his compulsion? A regular vampire could compel a few people at once; a powerful one could compel a whole room.

No, they must have left for another reason. If my sire really had dismissed the whole building ... he was deadlier than deadly.

I didn't want to think about that.

"Think about home," I murmured to myself as I took the stairs to ground level far too fast, overbalancing at the bottom and having to grab the wooden newel post to stop myself hitting the floor teeth-first.

"Just think about home," I reminded myself, picturing my bed and imagining diving into the cushions, swaddling myself in the duvet's scent of lavender and safety.

"Okay," I breathed, walking swiftly past the place where I'd died and burst back to life, trying not to think of the terrifying moments in between. "Everything's going to be okay. I'm going home."

But I didn't know where my sire had gone, or why he'd turned me, or what I was going to do.

Or if he'd come back for me.

FOUR

THE DOOR SQUEAKED WHEN I LET MYSELF INTO MY house, my whole body trembling. I tried to convince myself it was the cold making me shake and not a strange cocktail of adrenaline, terror, and trauma.

"Karina?"

I jumped at Aunt Jubilee's smoky voice. *Get it together, Karina,* I growled at myself. *You're home, you're safe. It's just Aunt Jubilee.*

"Yeah?" I called back, taking my time hanging my coat up and removing my boots, regular mundane actions to ground myself. I was home, I was safe, there were no vampire attackers lurking here.

I flinched at the thud of movement, but exhaled roughly a moment later when the huskies bounded into the hall to smother me with love and fur. I laughed, expelling a tiny bit of anxiety, as they laid into me with high pitched yowling for being gone so long.

"I know, I know, I'm awful."

Their replies wholeheartedly agreed.

"Kitchen," Aunt Jubilee called.

I pushed off my shakiness, threw my shoulders back, and walked confidently into the kitchen, the dogs glued to my side. I kept my eyes averted so Jubilee didn't spot anything different with my irises, and I made sure every movement was slow, nothing even remotely near vampire speed.

"Here, take this casserole," Jubilee said without preamble, putting an overfull bowl of food in my hands before I could speak. "You need to eat, I can sense it."

Aunt Jubilee was a seer like me. Or like I *had* been. She didn't see things in fractured shards like I did, but in her tarot cards and runes, and her sixth sense was a thousand times better than mine. I prayed she couldn't sense I was dead.

I swallowed hard, covering up my grimace with a smile as the smell of chicken stock and cooked vegetables reached my nose and made my stomach roil.

"Thanks," I replied, my smile still stuck in place. "I'm starving."

Aunt Jubilee gave me a scrutinising look; I fixed my gaze on my food and endured her all-seeing stare. I really, really didn't want to eat it. Just the thought of it made me nauseated, and that made me feel even worse. Aunt Jubilee's food was my favourite; I had her casserole at least once a week. But it was so unappetising to me now that bile hit my throat.

Maybe if she spiked the gravy with blood...

No. I went cold at the thought.

"You look pale, Karina," Jubilee said finally, stepping closer so her purple velvet dress—decked out in dark beads and glittering sequins—caught the edge of my vision. "Eat. You'll feel better."

I had no doubt I would, but I wouldn't be eating any time soon. Not with what my new body demanded.

"This smells great," I said, sidestepping her and heading across the black-and-white tiles for the cutlery drawer, glad for a chance to hide my face. Did I look monstrous? Was I hideous now, so obviously a vampire that I didn't even look like myself anymore? I should have found a mirror at the library. I was so stupid to come home and expect everything to go back to normal.

"Where's mum?" I asked, hunting down a spoon and hoping Jubilee didn't hear the too-fast, scratchy quality of my voice. "Still at work?"

"You know your mum," Aunt Jubilee replied easily, as if she hadn't noticed something was off with me. My shoulders sagged in relief. "Busy, busy bee. Watch out for a blond man," she added, making me stiffen. "My cards said he's dangerous."

My mouth dried. "A blond man?" I echoed, taking a tiny spoonful of casserole and fighting the urge to gag as I swallowed a sip of gravy. This was impossible. How was I going to keep up this ruse? Vampires didn't eat; I knew that. I hadn't realised we *couldn't* eat because food smelled disgusting.

"Well, no worries," I said, aiming a smile in Aunt Jubilee's vague direction. I could hear her heartbeat, where mine was silent, could smell her powdery lilac perfume and the lily of the valley talc she'd used this morning, every one of my senses heightened. "I don't know any blond men."

"No boyfriend then?" Jubilee pushed, making me laugh.

"No chance of that, don't worry." I dared a glance up, and smiled at the sceptical look on Aunt Jubilee's face. "Really, I'm not dating anyone."

Her kohl-lined eyes narrowed. "I see another man in your future, Karina."

"You always see a man in my future," I teased, a weight sliding off my shoulders at the normality of the moment. "You've been saying that for years."

"And I've been seeing a man in your future for years," she replied firmly, but her mouth flicked up at the edges. "Come have a reading."

"No," I protested, backing towards the door with the casserole I needed a secret way to dispose of. No way was I hurting my aunt's feelings by refusing her food. "No, I'm good. I don't need to know what's in my future."

I already had a good enough idea: blood, death, and an unhealthy amount of terror.

The blond man she'd seen had to be the same man I had a gauzy memory of. My sire—he had to be.

"I'm sensing tall, dark, and handsome, too," Jubilee taunted, crossing her arms over her velvet dress, and giving me a smirk. "You sure you don't want to know what's in store?"

"Definitely not," I disagreed with a forced laugh, reaching the door. "I'm good with not knowing."

Jubilee shrugged, batting frazzled red hair out of her eye. "Well if it was me getting a hunk delivered to me, I'd want to savour every moment."

I groaned in embarrassment—and then a deeper, involuntary groan when the thump of her blood quickened, filling all my senses until I could hear nothing else. "I'm going up to my room," I rushed out. "See you in the morning."

I couldn't hear my voice over the whoosh of her blood, couldn't hear her reply, either, but I watched my aunt nod. Concern furrowed her brow as I escaped into the hall, taking long, deep breaths to clear my senses and beyond relieved that the huskies didn't follow me out. Maybe they sensed the change in me now.

My fangs ached, throbbing. But I wasn't *hungry*. I wasn't overwhelmed by a demanding thirst. I wasn't anything like the stories of vampires.

Clutching the casserole I had no intention of eating, I sped upstairs—far too fast, and elegantly enough that not a single drop of gravy spilled—where I retreated into my room.

It wasn't a comfort like I'd imagined it would be. The half-finished painting taunted me, reminding me I wasn't the same person who'd started creating them. The bed was an empty promise because I didn't need to sleep.

Could I sleep? Or like eating, would it be repulsive to me?

My bottom lip wobbled, and bloody tears stabbed my eyes as I crossed the soft carpet to put my uneaten food on the table by the window. I couldn't keep pretending forever, but I needed more time. The thought of Aunt Jubilee and Mum finding out someone had transformed me into the living dead ... it made more tears well in my eyes and drip down my cheeks.

I hastily ripped a tissue out of the box on my bedside table—when reading, they were always necessary—and mopped up the blood before it could mar my carpet. The coppery scent made my nose sting, blotting out every other smell, but there was no way to silence the sounds I could hear around me, all the way to the end of the street. And nothing softened the wild sensitivity of my skin, the brush of cotton on my arms getting more abrasive with every minute.

Aunt Jubilee was still downstairs, but heavy footsteps

drifted up to my ears as she went into her tarot room and began to shuffle cards. Would she read for me tonight? What would she see?

My stomach knotted. I mopped up my crimson tears with the tissue and climbed into bed. Even if I couldn't sleep, at least I was somewhere familiar; at least I was safe here.

But I'd always felt safe at work, too.

I turned onto my side, staring emptily at the window, at the rows of roofs and houses that stretched across London. Somewhere in this dark, secretive city, was someone else going through what I was? Had someone else transitioned against their will and been left alone?

I buried my face in my hands and let out the sob that had been building for hours.

What was I going to do when everyone found out I was a vampire? It wasn't like the old days when the orders were at each other's throats, but my life would never be the same. I'd have to live in a nest of vampires, at least while I acclimated. I'd be torn away from my home, monitored to make sure I was safe, a council member watching over my every move.

Another sob tripped out and I curled up tight in my bed, knowing everything was about to change.

FIVE

THE DREAM WAS FULL OF BLOOD.

A whole river of it, flowing and rushing around me. Hot and seductive, it urged me to let go of the branch I clung to, fighting its violent flow. Blood was all I could smell, all I could feel splashed on my skin, soaking into my clothes and weighing me down.

There were people in the river, some screaming, trying to keep their heads above water. Above *blood*. Others ... not screaming, but pursuing the others. Hunting. Every few seconds, a scream cut out with a wet, gurgling sound, and my grip on the branch grew weaker.

Copper and iron coated my senses, and my mouth watered. I wanted to let go. That was the hardest part of holding on; I *wanted* to fall into the river of blood. I wanted it to carry me away, wanted to be consumed by it.

But if that happened, I knew I'd lose myself. I'd lose Mum, Aunt Jubilee, and my best friend. I'd lose the library, my job, and my calling. I'd lose any chance of proving to my family that I wasn't like my convict sister.

I dug my fingernails into the bark and held on tighter, but the river rushed faster.

"No," I breathed when my fingers slipped, blood splashing up my wrist as someone in the river was knocked into me, screaming for help.

I couldn't help them; they were washed away before I could even try. My heart crashed against my ribs as my fingers slid further down the branch.

"Please," I rasped, digging my fingernails into the bark and holding on with everything I had left. If I let go, if I fell into the river, it would swallow me whole and there'd be nothing left of me.

The part of me that wanted that to happen shuddered with glee, and cold tripped down my spine.

All it took was one more swell of rapid-flowing blood, and the branch slipped through my fingers. For a moment, I was weightless, floating, and serene. But then my head went under the water—under the blood—and all I heard was screaming.

It was my own voice.

SIX

I shot upright in bed with my breathing racing a mile a minute and an emptiness in my chest where my heart should have been hammering like a parade of drummers. It was still dark outside my window. My hands shook when I lifted them to my face and scrubbed my cheeks, my stinging eyes.

"Just a dream," I whispered, voice scratchy. "It's normal to have nightmares, especially with what happened today. It's just a dream. Just a dream."

But it was impossible to forget the way my heart had leapt when I fell into the river, or the relief I'd felt when the blood swallowed me, that moment of serene calm. For that split second I'd been content, and I *hated* it.

My teeth ached, distended fangs throbbing, and that only made my eyes sting harder. That fucking dream, the blood, the screams ... it had woken the dark parts of me that I wanted to sleep forever.

"Shit," I hissed, throwing back the covers and wincing at the deep, throaty quality of my voice. The soft cotton scratched my skin like sandpaper and I clenched my teeth—

and bit through the end of my tongue, filling my mouth with blood that only made my fangs ache fiercer.

My throat was desperately sore, like someone had taken a cheese grater to it while I slept. There was no pretending that I wasn't hungry. Thirsty.

"I can't do this," I rasped, scrubbing a shaky hand down my face. I couldn't drink blood, couldn't attack someone every time I got thirsty. This was ridiculous.

I knew the Shadow Order kept blood on hand, but I could only access that if I was registered with a vampire den. I selfishly wanted to pretend I was a normal seer for a while longer. Once I registered, everything became real. I'd be officially a vampire in the eyes of every order. I wouldn't belong in Light with my family anymore. Leona had done a lot of sketchy, dark things, but she'd never changed her biology and species.

Not that I'd done this to myself.

Ugh, I needed to tell someone, report it to the orders so they could make sure it didn't happen to anyone else. But not yet. Not tonight.

Dragging a ragged breath into my lungs, I grabbed my coat and shoved my feet into my shoes. It took me two attempts to fasten the laces; my fingers wouldn't stay still. I had to get out of here, get some fresh air, and calm my hunger. I didn't trust myself in the same house as Mum and Aunt Jubilee like this. Assuming Mum had actually come home from work; she'd been known to sleep in her office.

It was no effort at all to creep out of my room and down the stairs out the front door; my new, changed body moved as fast as a puma and as lightly as a feather over the creaky boards and groaning steps. Not even Jubilee's cats or huskies pricked their ears at my exit.

But I was too tense to appreciate my new talents, strung

tightly enough that I flinched at a dog barking down the street when I stepped outside.

"It's a dog," I hissed at myself, filling my lungs with biting night time air. I waited for the cold to raise goose bumps on my arms. It took me a few seconds to realise I couldn't feel the cold at all; it was like stepping outside on a balmy summer day.

"Vampire, Karina, remember?" I whispered, carefully closing the gate behind myself and setting off down the street towards the pungent scent of the Thames. I'd always loved the smell of the water, no matter how sharply it reeked, because it meant home. Now, I could smell it even stronger, and could taste every individual layer that made up the scent. It wasn't particularly pleasant.

"Okay," I breathed, coaching myself down from the panic as I walked, the cold helping to ease the throb in my fangs the longer I spent out here. It took effort to walk slowly instead of moving at crazy speed, but it was worth it for the clarity I felt as I turned onto the walkway beside the river.

I wanted to text Ruby, wanted to tell my best friend everything, but I wasn't brave enough. Not yet. Tomorrow— that was my new motto. I'd do it tomorrow, scouts' honour.

Besides, Ruby had been on a date tonight, and she'd been so excited; I didn't want to burst her post-date bubble of happiness if it had gone well. Tomorrow—I'd definitely phone her tomorrow.

Wind lifted the hair off the back of my neck, and I shivered at the sensation more than the chill as I followed the riverside path. The longer I sucked in air, the less my throat ached, and the better I felt.

I leant against the cold steel railing and let the wind drag my hair out behind me as I bowed over the rail to look into the river. My new sight could make out the individual ripples of water in the dark, every defined ring that formed as the breeze played with the river.

I was a vampire. A fucking *vampire*.

My eyes stung, and in the dark I let the tears fall, my nose full of the scent of coppery blood.

I didn't know *how* to be a vampire, how to feed or take care of myself or if I could still work at the library. What would happen if I went out during the day without a spelled bracelet? I'd never seen a vampire burst into flames; the rumours could be exaggerated.

Or I could be confined to the dark for the rest of my life.

Blood dropped into the Thames as reality finally settled in, hopelessness like a crushing weight on my chest. I knew logically I'd find a way to live with this—it wasn't like I had any other choice—but right now it seemed impossible.

I was supposed to be a normal seer for the rest of my life, and I wasn't even a very good one. I couldn't see anything days or weeks ahead like some seers, I didn't have a sixth sense like Aunt Jubilee, and I didn't always know what the fragmented shards of my vision were trying to tell me. But that *should* have been my biggest worry, not the crippling fear that I'd go home and hurt my fucking family.

Why did that blond vampire turn me? And why *leave* me?

I wiped tears off my cheeks and stared into the river, wishing I was brave enough to text Ruby or to call Mum. But the second they found out, my life would be divided into Before Transition and After Transition.

I didn't want my life to be over.

"'Scuse me, darling," a male voice called, making me jump.

I hastily wiped my cheeks free of tears, and hoped the dark would cover up the redness in my eyes when I turned.

"I hate to ask," said a brown-haired man in his thirties. He wore a scruffy coat and combat boots, and wrung his hands in front of himself. "But do you have a pound to spare? I don't have enough for the bus fare home."

I frowned, looking closer at him. "Steve, you live at the end of my street, and it's two minutes away."

His hand wringing stopped instantly, his posture changing from hopeless to confident. "Oh, hey there, Karina. How's it goin'?"

"Ehhh."

How did you explain to someone that you'd been attacked and turned into a vampire, but had no memory of it, and you didn't know what the hell you were supposed to do with your life anymore? I stuck with 'ehhh.'

"Same here," he agreed with a rueful smile, angling closer. Steve was a charmer and a conman, but he was a nice enough neighbour and he'd helped raise money for Mrs Kang down the road when she needed specialist surgery on her hip. As far as people went, he wasn't the worst, but my defensive instincts kicked in with a sudden surge and I inhaled sharply at the force of it. The need to push him away, to hiss in his face, was so strong that I couldn't stop my upper lip curling off my teeth.

"Woah, there," he said, backing up a step in surprise.

The damage was already done. My already heightened senses amplified until all I could hear was a quickening thud-thud, until sweetness filled my nose and curled around my tongue. I could already taste it, and my fangs ached so much worse than earlier.

I stumbled back a step, panic making my breathing race. But it was exactly like my dream; I was clinging hopelessly to the branch, trying to avoid the rapid flow of the river. And like in my dream, I lost my grip and my head plunged below the surface.

"Karina?" Steve asked, a furrow between his brow as he backed up another step.

I moved so fast he didn't even see me coming. So fast I barely processed the movement myself. His shoulders felt strangely breakable in my grip, like I could shatter his bones with the slightest application of pressure. The thought horrified me, sending a shudder down my spine. Or maybe that was the way his heart thumped faster, filling his body with the scent of sweetness and sin. It was better than anything I'd smelled before, so strong it coated my tongue, promising a taste even better than this mere hint of it.

My head snapped forward, instinct controlling me like a puppet, and my throbbing fangs punctured thin skin. Horror curdled my stomach for a split second as I realised what I'd done. But then hot liquid poured over my tongue and I groaned, deep and loud, and there was nothing in my mind except the ambrosia sliding down my throat and how to get more and more and *more*.

The wind brushed over my skin like a sharp caress as I gulped and licked and swallowed, mindless with euphoria.

Holy fuck, this was amazing. Chills covered my arms, and my senses grew even clearer, until I swore colours glowed like stars in the air around me. I needed more, needed this to never stop. I knew when it did, there'd be nothing but darkness, and I couldn't bear it.

The more I drank, the better I felt, and I couldn't get enough—but rough hands grabbed my arms and wrenched me away before I could take another gulp.

I hissed on instinct, purely animalistic as I fought the ironclad grip, desperate to get back to the heavenly drink—

to chase the pleasure and promise in its taste and escape the darkness for a little bit longer.

But the grip didn't ease on my biceps no matter how hard I fought. Instead, I was turned in their grip as if I were a kitten fighting a lynx—diminutive and harmless.

"Stop," a hard male voice commanded, so powerful that I swore it sent ripples through the whole damn city.

I froze, my mouth slamming shut hard enough to slice through my bottom lip. Even my breathing hitched.

The rush faded, my mind clearing, and instead of euphoria, icy fear slushed through my body.

Who the hell was this man?

With my senses heightened, even in the dark I saw a powerfully built body, a devastating face that was all angles and harshness, and deep ruby eyes. I'd never seen him before, but there was no mistaking he was a vampire. Maybe he'd been at the library when I was attacked? Maybe he'd come to help—or to finish me off? Had turning me been a mistake he was meant to correct?

"You've made a damn mess," he growled, looking beyond me at—

Oh god. Steve.

I'd—I'd killed him, hadn't I?

I'd ripped out his throat and drank every drop of blood in his body like a monster.

Maybe I deserved to be snuffed out.

But every part of me screamed at the idea of death, and I lurched away from him, willing to jump into the damn river if that got me to safety. But my body didn't budge; not even my little finger so much as twitched.

Stop, he'd said. And I had.

Compulsion—a vampire's secret power. But if he'd compelled me, that meant he was unthinkably powerful.

Only the most dangerous, the *extremely* lethal, could compel other vampires.

Inside I shook and fought and screamed; outside, my body had frozen like an ice sculpture.

"More shit for me to clean up," the mystery vampire muttered, and returned his gaze to me.

My heart jumped and raced, trying to escape. I couldn't look away, forced to endure his piercing stare. Blood ran down my chin, the taste of it still coating my mouth. But instead of making my eyes roll back in pleasure, it made me sick.

I'd greedily sucked down blood, had swallowed enough that my stomach was *full* of it.

"It never fucking ends," he muttered, glaring at my slack face. "First the attacks in the east end, and now you."

I inhaled sharply, desperately trying to wrench away from him, begging my body to move. Was this the vampire who'd attacked all those people across the city? Was he going to do that to me, too?

"Who are you?" he demanded, clearly not expecting an answer—he'd compelled me to silence and stillness. "Why you?"

I'd been asking myself that since the moment I'd been reborn. Why me? What had I done to deserve this—any of it, all of it?

His piercing stare shredded my soul, as if he was scouring through everything that made me *me*. "You can tell me that when you wake up."

Wake up?

No, I tried to cry, to scream. I threw myself against the cage of my body, desperate to move, to escape. I thought he'd kill me, but kidnapping me suddenly seemed far fucking scarier, with a hundred more terrifying possibilities.

Let me go, I wanted to shout, to beg—whatever it took for him to let me go.

But the vampire just sighed, deeply exasperated, and his compelling voice rocked through me again when he commanded, "Sleep."

I thrashed inside my body, but there was no fighting his compulsion. It pressed on my eyelids, wrapped around my body like a fist, and crushed me into unconsciousness.

SEVEN

I SAT UP IN A DIZZYING RUSH, A DEEP HISS IN MY throat. I sounded like the cats who fought outside my bedroom window during the night; I didn't sound human.

My hiss twisted into a choked cry when reality smacked into me. I didn't sound human because I *wasn't* human. I'd been attacked, and turned. I was a fucking vampire, and I ... I'd killed Steve.

"You slept like the dead," a low, gravelly voice drawled. "Pun intended."

I jolted away from the voice, my eyes flitting around a small, cramped cell made entirely of stone except for ten steel bars. My back met an unyielding wall, and breath rushed out of me in a panic. I might have been a vampire, but apparently I wasn't impervious to fear.

"Who are you?" I demanded in a guttural voice, not recognising the sound at all. I dragged air into my lungs, tasting damp stone and stale water.

I was in a dungeon, trapped by iron bars and stone I had no hope of breaking through—even as a new vampire—and lounging on a plastic chair in the hallway outside my cell was the man who'd compelled me unconscious.

He tilted his head, watching me, and a few long, inky strands of hair fell from his messy bun, splaying across his cheek. I avoided his gaze, knowing just how easily he could compel me. But ... had I even locked eyes with him when he'd compelled me? I couldn't remember, but if I hadn't, he was even more powerful than I'd realised. Only the elite, top two percent could compel without eye contact.

I was going to die here, in this musty dungeon, with a vampire I didn't even know.

"Lazarus Kaine," he said, his rough voice making me jump. It took me a second to realise he was answering my question—*who are you?*

"Great, thanks," I snapped, my nerves completely frayed. "That really clears things up."

I pulled my knees to my chest, my hands shaking as I locked them together. It wasn't smart to show him how terrified I was, but I didn't give a shit. I didn't know why he'd grabbed me, why I was a vampire, or what he was going to do with me. Showing weakness was the least of my concerns.

Lazarus laughed, a soft huff of breath. "And who are you?"

"The woman you kidnapped," I replied, as sharp as my breathy voice could sound.

I shook so hard that the bed rattled beneath me, drawing my attention to the metal frame and surprisingly adequate mattress. I'd been so distracted by the dungeon and the vampire, I hadn't even noticed what I'd laid on.

"The woman I stopped slaughtering her way through half of London," he countered, an eyebrow raised in superior judgement. He looked unaffected by the fact he'd kidnapped me.

I dug my fingernails into my palms. I couldn't deny his accusation. I didn't know what I'd have done after I ... after I killed Steve. Would I have found another person to drain blood from, and then another, and another?

"Gods," I choked out, and buried my face in my shaking hands. Choked sounds clawed their way up my throat. Blood filled my senses as my eyes stabbed with tears, but I fought them back; I couldn't see anything but red when I cried, and being blind around a strange vampire would get me killed.

"You can start with your name, that's easy enough," he said, making me jump.

I snapped my head up and glared at my kidnapper. I should have been playing nice, making friends, reminding him that I was a person with opinions and dreams and a family who'd missed me—basic kidnappee protocol—but terror made my tongue sharp.

"Why do you give a shit about my name? Is this a sick trophy thing? You collect the names of the people you kidnap?"

He rolled dark red eyes, giving me a *look* like I was being ridiculous.

"I could call you baby vamp if you'd prefer," he said with an arch smile, propping his foot on his opposite knee as he leaned back. Lazy, sardonic, amused—amused by me being locked *in a fucking dungeon*.

My blood sparked and burned. "If you *must* know, my name's Karina. What were your other victims called?"

"What was *your* victim called?" he fired back, blunt enough that I flinched. "How were you turned, Karina?"

I laughed bitterly, the sound echoing off the stone walls

and taunting me with an audience of laughter. "Good fucking question."

He watched me long enough that I squirmed on the bed, goosebumps tumbling down my arms. I was still wearing my skirt and cardigan from work for gods' sakes, blood blending in with the pattern on my arm and dust from falling books ingrained in the wool.

"You don't know how you were turned?" he observed, tilting his head in the opposite direction. I got the sense of being watched by a vulture, and my stomach twisted.

"There's a gap in my memory," I explained, mostly because I needed to tell someone, and there were no consequences of telling this stranger unlike telling my friends and family. "There's a man, a face, and that's it. I don't know what happened to me."

"Do you have a bite?" Lazarus asked, his intensity sharpening as he set both feet on the ground and leaned forward, his eyes fixed on me.

I swallowed, not sure why he cared—or why he hadn't made any demands of me yet, because he *clearly* wanted something. I rolled up my cardigan sleeve and showed him where blood had dried on my skin. There was no scratch there anymore, but there was no missing where it had been.

"I was scratched," I said quietly, looking at my blood-streaked arm. I curled my hand into a fist and watched the tendons move beneath my skin. I knew this cell must have been icy cold, but I couldn't feel the temperature at all. "But then I died, and ... it's gone."

"Tell me everything you remember," Lazarus demanded, his red eyes sharp and fixed on me. Predatory, but ... desperate, too.

"Why?"

I swallowed when his stare snapped up to my face, my

instincts bleating that he was impossibly dangerous. He could kill me before I'd even blinked—even *with* my new vampire speed.

But why did he care so much about my transition?

Lazarus's mouth pressed into a flat line, accentuating the harsh angles of his pale face. "Do you want to learn how to control your feeding instinct? I can teach you, so you'll never have to kill anyone ever again."

I opened my mouth to instantly agree, but I remembered that edge of need in his intensity. "What's the catch?"

Lazarus leaned back in his plastic chair, a shrewd glint in his ruby eyes as he crossed big arms over his chest, his black shirt straining at its buttons.

"You might not remember who turned you, but there's a link between the two of you—progeny and sire. I want you to use it to find him. That's all."

I barely suppressed a scoff, suspicion churning through me. I didn't believe his 'that's all' for a damn second.

But it sounded like that was the only way I was getting out of this dungeon.

"If I refuse?" I asked, braced for a threat.

There was nothing soft and kind about Lazarus Kaine; he was pure darkness and violence. The epitome of a vampire. I doubted he'd ever show me mercy.

"If your sire isn't found, and stopped, the council will send their shadowhounds after him—*and* all his progeny."

Now I felt the cold, a chill travelling through me. Everyone knew about the shadowhounds; never seen but always feared, they hunted down supernatural criminals and turned them to blood and ash.

Lazarus's pause made my anxiety spike.

He finished, "And you'll be executed along with them."

EIGHT

Unless I helped this lethal stranger find the man who'd attacked me, the council's most terrifying executioners would hunt me down and turn me to dust? What the fuck?

"Why do you want to find him so badly?" I asked finally, my mouth as dry as a desert despite the blood still dried around my mouth—and sitting heavily in my belly.

Lazarus scoffed.

I got to my feet in an effortless rush of motion, crossing my arms over my chest and hiding my shaking hands. "Don't bullshit me. You *need* to find the man who attacked me."

"Your sire," he corrected with a wry, knowing look.

I avoided that.

"If you expect me to help you, I want to know *why*," I insisted, curbing the need to pace the slabs of stone that made up the floor. But fuck, it was hard; the compulsion to pace made my soles itch.

Lazarus snorted. "If you don't want to be slaughtered by the hounds, you'll help me. And like I said, I'll teach you to manage your thirst. From the good of my heart," he added in a sardonic voice.

"So kind of you," I replied in the same tone, my blood boiling hotter. I'd been killed, turned, and now the shadowhounds would kill me *again* because of who'd attacked me—and Lazarus sounded so fucking *amused* by all of it.

I wanted to punch his smug face and break his nose. Judging by the wonky set of it, someone had beat me to the punch. Pun intended.

"I try," he drawled, the corner of his mouth flicking into a smirk sharper than any blade. "You can leave, of course. I'll let you out, you can continue your murderous rampage through London, expose all vampirekind—and potentially all *supernatural*kind—and then you'll get executed in a month by the hounds."

Lazarus shrugged a muscular shoulder. "Completely up to you, Karina."

I hissed, that fighting-cat sound again. Sure, I could leave. If I wanted to become a serial killer.

"Wait," I breathed. "What do you mean *a month?*"

"Yeah, that's the best part," Lazarus said, deadly still as he watched me. "I have until the end of the year to find your sire."

It was December 2nd when I'd been turned. Gods knew what the date was now; how long had I been knocked out by Lazarus's compulsion?

"So what'll it be?" he asked, his earlier intensity returning Ashe pinned me with a stare. "Will you help me, or wait for the shadowhounds to kill you?"

It was no choice at all. I *hated* it, but the only thing I could possibly say was, "I'll help you."

NINE

"You said *you* have until the end of the year to find my attacker. Why you?" I demanded, watching Lazarus.

"You don't need to know that," he replied dismissively. But there was something in the way his red eyes tightened, a secret he was holding onto tightly, and my distrust increased. "The only thing that matters is unless your sire is brought to heel—and presented to the council—before the end of the year, your life will be cut short."

"You expect me to trust you, that easily?" I asked with a rusty laugh. "I don't think so, buddy."

"I'm trusting *you*, aren't I?" he retorted, a dark eyebrow raised. "Someone I found fangs-deep in someone's throat just hours ago."

I physically flinched away from the ugly truth, and watched him notice it. "You said you'd teach me control."

Lazarus linked his fingers on his knee and leant back in the plastic chair, looking like a haughty lord even with the damp and dungeon. This cell was a damn strange setting for someone so dangerously attractive, and for someone wearing a shirt and trousers that looked finer than anything I'd worn—or *seen*—in my life.

"I'll teach you, but whether it works depends on you," he replied, watching me back. "It'll be useless unless you face the truth of what you are."

I pressed my mouth into a thin line, my arms crossed tight over my chest. I allowed myself to pace two steps, just to take the edge off. "If I wanted a therapist, I'd have gone to one."

Lazarus did that infuriating head tilt again, strands of dark hair spilling into his face, making him even hotter. I tried not to notice how attractive he was, tried to focus on the threat he posed, but it was difficult not to see both at the same time. "Something tells me you and therapists are like oil and water."

"Oh, because you know me so well," I laughed, a dark thing made throatier by a hiss I didn't intend to make. "Teach me to control my thirst, and then let me out. I'm going home."

"To murder your parents?" he asked mildly, amusement bright in his eyes when I bared my teeth. "Feel free. I'll even open the cell for you."

He rose to his feet.

I gritted my teeth and called him on his bluff. He'd locked me here so I wouldn't hurt anyone else; he was hardly going to let me loose on my family.

"Go on, then," I challenged when he paused with his long fingers on a padlock bigger than my hand. "Open it up, I'm ready to leave."

Lazarus let out a heavy sigh. "I can already tell you're going to be a pain in the ass. Here." He turned and retrieved something from under his chair, and I jumped at the sight of him holding out a bag of *blood*, like I was waiting for a transfusion.

"You're joking," I said flatly, staring at the proffered bag and not even *thinking* of accepting it. "What Vampire Diaries nonsense is this? I'm not having that; someone might need it. Give it back to the hospital."

Lazarus's expression flattened in disbelief. "You're a nightmare."

"Says the vampire powerful enough to compel another vampire," I retorted, my blood sparking hotter.

"Drink or don't. If you'd rather be left with the taste of lifeblood in your mouth, suit yourself. But you'll want more. They always do."

He let his hand drop, and despite everything I said, my eyes followed that bag, my fangs throbbing. I ignored all of it, all the signs that I was no longer myself.

"Either way, you're going to help me," Lazarus went on, his voice sharpening. "You'll lead me to your sire, and then I can be done with you."

"*Sorry*," I said with zero sincerity. "Is kidnapping and imprisoning a woman so troublesome for you? My sympathies."

A light sparked in his eyes; a muscle feathered in his jaw. "The blood's from the depository, not a hospital. You're not taking it from someone who needs it." He shrugged, turning away. "Let me know when you get hungry."

"Hey!" I launched myself at the bars, wrapping my hands around their metal. Warm—another sign that I was unnatural. "You can't just leave me here!"

Lazarus shrugged, not turning back. "Call this lesson one in mastering your thirst. Learn patience. If your fangs hurt too badly, feel free to chew on the bars." He threw a look over his shoulder, sardonic as hell. "They make excellent teething toys."

"*Lazarus!*" I screamed, hammering on the bars when he walked out of view.

I pricked my newly sensitive ears and heard his footsteps echo off the stone, and then pad softly over carpet until I couldn't hear him anymore.

"That bastard," I snarled, curling my hands into fists and pacing from one end of the cell to another.

He couldn't just *leave* me here.

Except he had.

TEN

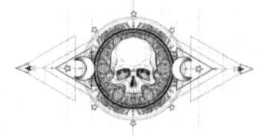

I fell into a fitful sleep, jerking awake at every sound my oversensitive ears picked up, my body locked in readiness of an attack. *Another* attack. I couldn't remember how I'd been turned, but that didn't stop me inventing scenarios, each one more gruesome and violent than the last.

I hadn't fallen off a ladder into the bookshelf, that was for sure. The vampire who'd turned me had done that. Pushed me? Thrown the bookshelf on top of me, hoping it would kill me after he scratched me?

I must have dozed for a few minutes because I startled awake with a hiss, my breathing spiralling in response to a deep, primal panic.

"Easy," a man murmured. It took me a second to remember Lazarus, his proposal, and our bargain—help him find my attacker, and he'd teach me not to be a serial killer. Oh, and as a bonus the shadowhounds wouldn't snuff my life into nothing.

"Oh, it's you," I said sourly, scraping sleep from my eyes

—why were my eyes worse after shitty sleep than when I slept deeply?—and climbing off the bed.

Lazarus was unchanged from whenever he'd last come to gloat at me: his black hair was pulled into a bun, his face sharp-planed and intense, softened only by the glittering amusement in his deep red eyes. I purposefully didn't look at the way his shirt clung to his biceps and chest, or the way his trousers hugged his shapely backside. I had enough problems without getting the hots for my abductor.

Although ... he'd abducted me to stop me hurting anyone else. And I couldn't help but feel a little bit grateful for that.

"Sorry for taking so long," he said, the corner of his mouth curving and a dimple appearing in his cheek. Ugh, he had a dimple? Who decided vampires could have dimples? "I had to baby-proof the house."

It took me a second to grasp his meaning—I was the fucking baby—and then I bared my teeth, putting all my frustrated, edgy emotions into a guttural hiss.

Lazarus just smirked, watching me from the other side of the bars, his hands in the pockets of his black trousers and his posture confident, unbothered.

"Since you're too stubborn to feed from a blood bag, I had to make sure you wouldn't break out of the house to find a snack."

My face stung—not a flush, no heat crept into my cheeks, but something like it—and I averted my gaze. "I won't hurt anyone else."

"You don't *want to*," he replied, something unknowable in his voice as he watched me, his gaze burning. "There's a difference."

I watched closely as he reached into his trouser pocket and

pulled out an old iron key, fitting it to a lock on my dungeon cell. For a split second, I contemplated drawing on all my new speed and shooting past him the moment the bars swung open.

I tensed my muscles, my breathing coming faster with every second. My heart should have been thumping inside my ribs, but it was still, another reminder that I was dead.

"By all means," Lazarus drawled, turning the key. "Try to run. Try to be faster than a three-hundred year old vampire faster, stronger, and far more superior than you."

I stiffened, grinding my teeth, and hissed when I sliced through my tongue. Blood pooled in my mouth. Lazarus's smirk deepened as he swung the door open, sweeping his arm in a taunting gesture.

Well, if he was going to make it easy...

I launched myself at the opening with every bit of strength in my body, stunned by how easily I cut through the air, how strong my body was now.

But I veered too far to the left and slammed head-first into the solid bars of my cell, the impact reverberating through my skull with a deep ring.

"For fuck's sake, Karina," Lazarus growled, stalking into the cell and grabbing my face, tilting my head left and right while he glared at me. "You need training wheels."

I snorted, too disoriented to be pissed off. Besides, it was funny and he was right.

"I'm fine," I slurred, wrenching my face from his hands—surprisingly warm for a three-hundred-year-old vampire—and wobbling into the bars. Again.

"Yeah," he agreed, deadpan. "You look *fine*."

I scowled, rubbing my forehead where an ache pounded.

"Come on," he laughed, strong fingers wrapping firmly around my wrist. "You're coming upstairs."

"Can't kill me down here?" I replied sharply, blinking as my vision wavered on the first step out of the cell, my head pounding. "Is the ambience not right? Too damp and acrid?"

"I'm hardly going to kill you when I need you to find Lorn," he replied, giving me a sideways look as he led me down the row of cells toward a cramped staircase. This whole dungeon looked ancient, older than even Lazarus. "Why would I kill you when you're useful to me?"

I made a gruff sound, my head thumping. "I just walked into an iron bar, give me a break."

He snorted, pushing me in front of him as we ascended the steps, my nose picking up the scent of laundry and sandalwood. And were those fresh orchids?

"You look like I'm leading you to the gallows," he laughed. "I already said I'm not going to hurt you. You're useful to me."

"Because I can help you find *Lorn?*" I asked, emphasising the name he'd dropped—either intentionally or by accident.

"Exactly," he agreed. "Your sire. And my progeny."

I spun, surprise catching me off guard, to stare at Lazarus. My feet moved faster than I'd been expecting, and I would have toppled down the stone steps if Lazarus hadn't caught my shoulders and stabilised me.

"Your progeny? You mean your ... your *son* killed me?"

I wrenched out of his grip, grinding my fangs as a terrible anger shook inside me.

"That irresponsible *wretch* is not my son," Lazarus snarled, matching my anger. His face was transformed, hollows carved in his face and his eyes almost black as he bared his fangs at me. "I might have turned him, but he's no son to me."

"That's why the council are making you find him," I

realised, curling my fingers into fists. "Because he's your problem. You *made* him. And it's your fault that he hurt *me*. Who else has he attacked?" I asked, realisation sparking somewhere in my brain. "Are there others like me, who he's killed and left to be reborn?"

"No," Lazarus snarled. "Only you. But he's a problem for all of us, and if he isn't stopped, all three orders could be exposed. The last thing anyone wants right now is for humans to form a mob. Or worse, a fucking task force."

And they would. My blood chilled, my anger simmering instead of erupting.

"The attacks in the east end—those are him, too?"

"It seems that way," Lazarus agreed tightly, his face still sharp and skeletal as he brushed past me up the stairs. "But why he didn't do the same to you is a mystery."

I blinked through a bout of dizziness, pressing my hand to the wall as I followed Lazarus cautiously. What if he decided I was a problem for him, like Lorn? What if he decided it was easier just to kill me?

"I hate mysteries," Lazarus seethed under his breath, pushing open a heavy wooden door with a creak when he reached the top of the stone staircase.

More of that laundry powder and orchid scent hit my senses, and the mundane smell went some way to easing my fraught nerves. I wanted to go home with a force that made my chest hurt, but Lazarus was right about one thing. I couldn't trust myself around Mum and Aunt Jubilee after what I'd done to Steve.

I was lucky, so damn lucky, that I hadn't hurt Jubilee in the kitchen.

"What are you going to do with me?" I asked tentatively. "I know I'm supposed to help you find Lorn, but what else?

You better not expect me to serve you," I added, heavy on disgust.

Lazarus snorted, leading me out of the damp, stone-dominated dungeons into an opulent corridor. I stared at the rich décor and gilt-framed paintings, my boots sinking into a plush carpet that ran down the centre of the hallway. Everything was blood red or sapphire blue or deep forest green, from the curtains shutting out the sun to the fat crystals on the lampshades to the clothes of the austere men and women in the paintings.

It looked more like a museum than a house, but with a vampire living here, I supposed that was appropriate. Lazarus was old enough to be in a museum himself.

"Sex slavery isn't my style," he replied with an infuriating little smirk. "My partners come willingly. And often," he added with a wink.

I glared, ignoring the flicker of heat that moved through me. Who cared how handsome he was, or how provocative the wink was? He'd kidnapped me, and I needed to remember that.

He kidnapped you to stop you killing anyone else, that annoying inner voice reminded me. I shut it out.

"I highly doubt that," I said after a too-long pause. "You seem too full of yourself to consider anyone else's needs."

His smirk deepened into something darker. "It's my lovers who are full of me, Karina."

I blinked and he was in front of me, warm fingers skimming down my neck and making my breathing catch. I shoved him away in the next second, my expression dark and threatening, but there was no silencing that hitch in my breath or undoing my body's reaction. Damn him.

"I'm not interested," I bit out, and exhaled in relief when he moved out of my personal space without pushing me.

"You're missing out," he said, his smirk back in place. Ugh, why did it make him even sexier? I fixed my stare on one of the portraits, an ugly woman in an enormous collar scowling back at me. "And you *did* want my help with your hunger, after all. Sex helps. So does violence—sparring."

The look he threw my way dripped with self-assuredness. "Let me know whichever you choose, Karina. Either one will end with you, panting, on your back."

ELEVEN

I HISSED, DEEP AND VICIOUS IN MY THROAT, AND launched myself at Lazarus, wanting to knock the smug expression off his face. He caught both my wrists in one hand with a low laugh, brushing a strand of red hair behind my ear with another. He incapacitated me in a heartbeat, with no apparent effort. Bastard.

"I'm not saying this just to provoke you," he said with an annoying little smirk. "It's the truth—blood is the only cure for the thirst, but the satisfaction doesn't last. You'll need something to take the edge off."

"Then I'll fight you," I hissed, my breathing fast. I wasn't a hundred percent sure why I was so furious with him, only that he'd baited me, and I felt like an idiot for falling for it.

"Alright," Lazarus agreed pleasantly, letting go of my wrists and rolling up the sleeves of his sleek black shirt.

I fixated on the place where veiny, muscle-corded skin was revealed inch by inch, and had to shake myself out of it. Not now, arm kink!

"Fight me," he challenged.

He swept his arms out at his sides, feet braced evenly on

the carpet, looking like a dark gothic prince with his black hair, angular face, and intense eyes.

I didn't need telling twice.

I curled my hands into fists and threw a punch, my arm sailing through the air so fast it blurred. I was getting used to the speed, getting used to the shockingly graceful way my limbs moved—like water and air instead of flesh and bone—so I managed to actually direct my fist toward Lazarus' sharp jaw.

But he moved even swifter, knocking my hand aside.

"Aiming for my face?" he chided with a raised eyebrow. "And here I thought you'd have good manners. Chest and below only," he ordered.

No problem. I knew exactly where my next blow was going to land.

I gritted my teeth and threw my fist at his face again, distracting him so I could bring my knee up in a clumsy manoeuvre I'd seen on TV. He caught my wrist like I'd expected, but my knee slammed successfully into his crotch.

He grunted a satisfying curse, letting go.

"Right," he said in a choked voice, coughing out a laugh when he stepped back. "You play dirty. Good to know."

The grin I gave him was smug and a little bit mean. I didn't even know *why* I was furious at him. It wasn't his fault his progeny had attacked me. The person I was last year might have blamed him, but after everything with Leona and how mum took all that blame and responsibility on herself, I'd had a wake-up call. Or several.

I stepped away from Lazarus, watching him wince and curl his hands into fists.

"Feel better?" he asked, watching me as he flicked dark strands of hair from his eye and stood fully with effort.

I blinked, waiting for him to retaliate for the below-the-belt move, but he never did.

"I do," I answered a beat too late, bewildered. My blood wasn't boiling anymore, and my breathing had steadied a little.

"Good," he replied with a brisk nod, turning and heading down the corridor. "I'm already behind schedule."

I hurried to catch up—and ended up overshooting him by several feet in an expected burst of speed. Lazarus's laugh threatened to spark my temper again, but it wasn't condescending, which saved him another hit to the dick. It was a nice sound, gravelly and deep.

"Behind schedule for what?" I asked, maintaining pace with him with immense effort. I glanced at his sharp profile, unable to read his thoughts or emotions. Sometimes I thought he was irritated to have to deal with me, and sometimes I thought I amused him endlessly.

"Dinner," he responded, stalking around a corner and down a deep emerald hallway lined with honey-wood doors and vases towering with fresh flowers—orchids, like I'd smelled earlier.

It was nice—his home, lair, whatever this was. Austere and castle-like in parts, but with an obvious attempt to make it homely with brocade velvet curtains, thick carpets, glittering lamps and chandeliers, and art everywhere I looked. I wanted to pause by each portrait and landscape, wanted to analyse the more abstract pieces to search for a meaning within the strokes and swirling shapes.

"We can eat?" I asked with surprise, my eyes trailing over a portrait of a lonely-looking woman done entirely in blacks and greys except for a blazing red slash over her eyes. "I thought..."

Lazarus shot me a look both amused and sympathetic. "Did you try to eat after you were turned?"

I scrunched my nose at the memory of Jubilee's casserole. "No, but ... it smells..."

"Disgusting," Lazarus finished with another gravelly laugh. "Yeah, all food's like that. You can eat if you want to, but expect to throw it up minutes later. Some fledglings like to convince themselves it tastes the same as it did when they were living; feel free to join their ranks."

"No, thanks," I replied, my stomach whirling just at the thought. "So who's dinner for? Do you have guests?" Something occurred to me, and a chill swept through me. "Who else lives here? What if they decide I'm too much trouble and kill me—you'll never find Lorn then."

"Easy," Lazarus murmured, pausing on the threshold of a wide, airy kitchen with the shades pulled over every window. "No one's going to kill you. You're under my protection, so even if someone else did live here, you'd be beyond harm."

That wasn't too reassuring, given I didn't know who the hell Lazarus was beyond being old as fuck and the sire of my attacker. But at least Lazarus seemed inclined to let me live; I'd rather take my chances with him than someone else.

"Okay," I agreed, disturbed by the intense, searching look he was giving me.

"Who are you?" he asked, something softer about his voice as he watched me. "Beyond your name, who are you? How did you end up crossing paths with Lorn?"

I shrugged, throwing my hands up, beyond helpless and frustrated with it. "I don't know how. I have a vague memory of a face, and that's it. I'm a librarian, an archivist. I was waiting for a client to pick up—a book?"

I frowned, scouring my memory for the name of the

book and coming up empty. An ache throbbed behind my skull and I clenched my jaw.

"Was Lorn your client?" he pressed, but patiently, strangely considerate for a man who'd grabbed me, locked me in a cell, and laughed at my suffering.

"I have no idea," I huffed. "I don't remember anything; there's just a huge gap between waiting for my client and waking up in the archives room with the whole damn place falling down around me."

The black pit of my memory was like a broken tooth. I *had* to keep prodding it, couldn't stop myself.

"I'm just a librarian," I said, as if that could undo my transformation, as if the blond bastard would appear and say *so, sorry, I thought you were someone else, I'll change you back real quick.*

"I don't know why a vampire would attack me. I don't know what the hell I'm doing here."

Lazarus's shoulders heaved with a sigh, and he nodded, sweeping his hand out at the kitchen. "Come on, you can tell me everything you do remember, and I'll see if I can undo the compulsion."

Compulsion. The word rang through me like a bell struck. *Of course* I'd been compelled. Of-fucking-course. It made sense now, the block of memory missing. I'd been *told* to forget.

Lazarus stalked across the black and white checkerboard floor, looking comfortable among the charcoal cupboards and quartz worktops. Why did a vampire look so at home in a kitchen when he couldn't eat? I frowned at the edge of the kitchen, watching him ... pull an apron off a hook and tie it around his waist.

What?

I knew my expression must have been comical when

Lazarus began rifling through a fridge disguised as a cabinet, pulling out fresh vegetables and beef steak. It was so strange that I didn't even linger on my dread at having been compelled.

"There's wine in that decanter," he said, waving his hand absently at an opulently carved glass decanter sitting on the kitchen island. "Feel free to pour yourself a glass; it doesn't exactly help with the hunger, but it doesn't hurt, either."

He lifted his gaze from the chopping block between laying out florets of broccoli and a small army of asparagus and carrots. "You can spike it with blood if you're having a bad day. Or just pour blood into a glass and pretend it's wine," he added dryly.

I wrinkled my nose, the thought of drinking blood still abhorrent—but my mouth watered, and I couldn't quite shut out the memory of hot, unbelievably good liquid spilling over my tongue.

"I'll stick with wine," I murmured, suppressing a shudder. I couldn't tell if it was a shiver of revulsion or longing.

I slanted strange looks at Lazarus while I poured wine into a crystal glass I found beside the decanter, the three-hundred-year-old vampire calmly chopping up vegetables while a pan heated on the hob beside him. If no one else lived here, who was he cooking for? Or was it just a habit, left over from his living days?

"You said you could undo the compulsion?" I asked, sipping tentatively from my glass and surprised to find it tasted nothing like Aunt Jubilee's stew had smelled. The wine was *good*, actually, so I drank more. "How?"

"I'm older than Lorn," he explained, dropping the chopped vegetables into a frying pan. "More powerful. I could compel you to remember. There's a fifty-fifty chance it'll work, but it's better than nothing. Failing that, there are witches who might be able to undo it."

The strangeness of the domestic moment was impossible to ignore as he handled the pan like a chef, the apron tied around his waist clashing with his dark and dangerous aura. I sipped more wine, no idea what was happening. But at least I was out of the dungeon cell, and at least it smelled pleasant up here.

"Why would he compel me to forget?" I asked, voicing something that had bothered me since he'd spoken that word—compulsion. "What does it achieve?"

"You know something," Lazarus said seriously, meeting my gaze with a frown. My breathing hitched at the intensity of his stare, at the thrum of power and age around him.

My instincts screamed at me to run.

But if I ran, I'd go home. If I went home, I'd hurt Mum and Aunt Jubilee.

I wanted to be home more than anything, but I couldn't do that without knowing how to manage my hunger. A few throwaway comments about sparring and wine wouldn't stop me hurting someone else. Killing someone else.

I knew this was something I had to learn myself. I had to fight the thirst, however impossible that seemed. And no way was I fighting it anywhere remotely close to my family.

"I know lots of things," I replied finally, sullen as I slid onto a stool at the quartz island in the centre of the kitchen. "I can recite practically any line from Shakespeare or Chaucer. Ask me to name a hundred plants, and I can give you their botanical names. I know more random facts than I can ever hope to use in a single lifetime. But I don't see how that's of any use to a vampire."

Lazarus looked at me for a long second, measuring,

before he shrugged. It was such a normal gesture. "Neither do I. But we'll find out. It could help us find him."

I watched him add sliced meat to the pan in silence, draining the rest of my glass. *We'll find out.* It didn't sound like he was planning to drag the truth out of me, rather help me uncover it, but there was no way to know for sure. I could trust him to not kill me—while I proved useful—but that was all.

I mulled over the idea that I did know something, that I'd found something that a vampire would find useful—or want to keep quiet.

"There are a lot of dangerous books in the library," I said quietly, staring absently at the heavy curtains keeping out the sunlight. "Many of them are in the archives where I work."

Lazarus nodded, flipping cooked vegetables and meat onto a plate and arranging them *just so*. "That's a good place to start, then."

He crossed the kitchen to a small brass gong and, while I watched in disbelief, rang it with a low crash.

The response was instantaneous and bewildering: a high-pitched meow that grew louder the closer the cat came.

I blinked as a well-fed grey tabby trotted into the kitchen with their head at a proud tilt. They made short, hungry noises and aimed unerringly for Lazarus. The cat didn't even glance at me, as if I was beneath their notice.

"I know it's late," Lazarus apologised with a fond huff, placing the plate on a mat on the floor. "No need to shout at me. I was busy babysitting this one."

He jerked his chin in my direction, his conversation with the cat easy, casual, and with the air of something that happened often.

Lazarus, the vampire who'd compelled me unconscious and abducted me, had just spent twenty minutes lovingly preparing a homemade meal *for his cat.*

"What?" he demanded when he caught me looking at him. He narrowed dark red eyes, his biceps bulging in his black shirt when he crossed his arms over his chest.

"You must be pretty powerful if the council gave you a task," I said, glancing from him to the cat enthusiastically chowing down.

"I have a seat," he replied, watching me right back.

I blinked.

He ... he *sat* on the council? His status was that high? Holy hell.

"So you're a councilman," I laughed, turning the wine glass in my hand, "and you're a cat dad." I shook my head. "You're not what I expected."

If anything, his expression darkened rather than matching my amusement. "Come on, let Keith eat in peace. I'll see what I can do about removing that compulsion."

He stalked out of the kitchen at a fast clip, looking deadly and foreboding, but all I could do was shake my head.

Keith. His cat was called *Keith.*

TWELVE

I followed Lazarus up a grand, carpeted staircase to a second floor every bit as rich, opulent, and dark as the ground floor. Every curtain was pulled shut, and I was grateful; my day was bad enough without almost bursting into flames. Speaking of, I'd need to find a witch and bargain for a charm eventually. I couldn't live the rest of my life in the dark.

"Here's your room," Lazarus said in a gruff, gravelly voice. He paused outside a sturdy looking door in a corridor the same shade as the wine I'd drunk. I couldn't fault his interior decorating; it definitely fit the vibe I expected from a vampire.

"Thanks," I said awkwardly, hovering beside him when he opened the door, the musty scent of a room in need of airing out filling my senses. I felt somewhere between a prisoner and a guest, and I wasn't sure what to do next. Going into the room seemed like a no-brainer, but what did I do when I was there? Sit on the bed and stare into space?

I wanted to be home, but there was no way that could happen yet. When I'd got my vampire training wheels—and when the shadowhounds weren't going to hunt me down—I could go back, but for now I was stuck here. With a man I didn't know, in a house I was pretty sure was a mansion.

Going back to the Witching Library was suddenly far preferable to this awkwardness. Even if it was steeped in blood and dark memories, I knew my place there. I was good at my job, and I knew the people, knew exactly what to expect. My chest crushed like a solid weight pressed all the air out my lungs, but I bit the inside of my lip and didn't let my anxiety show.

What was I supposed to do? Just pretend everything was normal, become a vampire of leisure in between helping Lazarus track my attacker?

"I want my phone," I said suddenly, taking a hesitant step into the room. My eyes widened at the teal walls and the four-poster bed draped in blood red velvet to match the heavy curtains. "I know I had it when I went out last night, and I woke up without it, so you must have taken it. I want it back."

Mum and Aunt Jubilee would be panicking. Besides, I was supposed to meet my best friend for lunch, and there was no way Ruby hadn't blown up my phone with a hundred messages, morphing from demanding to confused to concerned.

"I wondered when you'd ask for it," he replied easily— and slid my phone from his pocket, the grey and pink cat case incongruous in his hand. I blinked when he passed it to me with no arguments. "I searched it for connections to Lorn, before you woke up."

"You searched my phone," I echoed, my expression darkening. The tips of my ears warmed at the thought of Lazarus reading the diary I kept in my notes, or scrolling through all the cute animal photos, book scans, and pieces of art in my camera roll. Let's not even talk about my hidden photos.

"I'm sorry," he said, crossing his arms over his wide chest and sounding unexpectedly genuine. "I wouldn't have invaded your privacy unless it was necessary. I thought you might be one of Lorn's thralls or blood donors, and I'd get an idea of his next move."

I mirrored his body language, ignoring my prickling face. "And what did you find?"

He shrugged. "A normal woman." He gestured me deeper into the room, studiously avoiding my gaze.

Great. Oh, that was *perfect*. My vampire abductor had, without a single doubt, seen the two photos I'd taken when I got new underwear and felt cute last month.

But if he wasn't going to acknowledge it, no way in hell was I voicing it.

"You should have everything you need in here," he said, his voice forcibly friendly. "There's a bathroom attached to this room, and a TV and radio if you get bored."

My eyes nearly popped out of my head. "There's a TV?"

None of the vampire lairs in my imagination had electricity, let alone a TV. If this place had Food Network and Sky Arts, I might survive this nightmare.

"There's a TV," Lazarus confirmed with a laugh, red eyes crinkling. "We're vampires, not cavemen."

"I thought they were one and the same," I said dryly, crossing the deep teal carpet to run my hand over the carved bed frame.

Lazarus watched me, his mouth curved sharply on one side. "Let me guess, you think all vampires run around in capes, turn into bats at night, and speak with a thick Romanian accent."

I shot him a dark look, trailing my hand along the bed covers. I wanted to climb in and sleep for a whole day.

"It's not my fault you keep to yourselves and the other orders know hardly anything about you. Half the stuff we hear could be rumour and superstition."

"And now you don't know which clichés are true, and what to expect from your own transition," he guessed. I didn't like the way he saw through my scowl to the insecurity beneath.

I ignored his penetrating stare, inspecting the bureau beside the window—giving the window itself a wide berth just in case the sun got any ideas about burning me.

Lazarus's gaze prickled my shoulder blades; I didn't like the sensation of being watched.

"We burn in the sun, that's true," Lazarus explained, somewhere between patient and ominous. "Garlic does nothing to repel us, but holy water stings like a bitch."

I snorted, more at the modern term in his mouth than the idea of being stung. "And crosses?"

"Terrified older vampires who were raised to be religious and believed they'd become corrupted by the devil. Some are still afraid of them, but most of us are nonplussed."

Great word—nonplussed. It was one of my favourites. I tried not to let it show, though. I was still undecided on Lazarus being a good guy or bad guy; he didn't need to know I liked his word choice.

"What about—sleeping in coffins?" I asked haltingly. I'd always hated coffins, the finality of them being nailed shut and dropped into the ground. I couldn't forget how Dad's coffin in the open maw of his grave, couldn't forget how much it hurt when they covered it with dirt.

"Depends on the vampire," Lazarus replied, this easy

offering of information surprising me. Wasn't he supposed to hold it hostage so I did whatever he told me to?

Maybe he was right, and my idea of vampires was outdated. Or maybe this was to get me to let my guard down, and then he'd strike while I was vulnerable.

"What about you?" I asked after a too-long pause, rifling through the drawers in the bureau to see what a vampire needed in their desk: ink, paper, pens, quills, and a blocky mechanical calculator.

"If you'd like to see where I sleep, Karina, I can certainly arrange it," he replied in a low purr. It slid along my senses like a warm breath.

I spun to face him with a hiss. "In your dreams, vampire."

His eyes crinkled when he laughed, the sound filling the room like music. "Cute insult. You're a vampire, too, Karina, whether you like it or not."

"Not," I said firmly.

"There are advantages," he replied, moving across the room towards me. He didn't move like a furious storm this time, but like a soft wind, elegant and sensual.

I straightened, swallowing at the shift in the atmosphere, at the softening of his expression.

"We're faster, stronger, and have sharper senses. That's why food is so unappealing; we can taste every layer of flavour."

"That sounds like a good thing," I pointed out, swallowing hard at the intensity on his face. Similar to his hunger to find Lorn, but also not. *Definitely* not. "Shouldn't food taste better?"

"In theory, yes. But our taste buds are too refined now. Everything that isn't blood tastes like dirt."

"Except wine," I countered, my skin prickling as he came closer, red eyes dark and sultry.

"Beer tastes vile," he told me. "Gin's passable."

Oh great, first Lorn killed me and *now* he'd taken beer from me, too? Wow.

"Everything is more heightened in this form," Lazarus went on, backing me up against the bureau and making my breath catch. "Touch is amplified, dreams are vivid, and we don't technically need to sleep. Which frees us up to fill our nights with whatever we decide."

"I'm not going to sleep with you," I said flatly.

"I know," he agreed, but his voice was still smoky and suggestive. "But there's a lot of space between chaste and carnal."

I jolted at his sudden movement, at the scrape of teeth up my throat, at the flash of icy fear and scalding lust that pounded through my body.

"I intend to explore that space," Lazarus murmured, his hand brushing lightly over my waist like a butterfly's touch —tantalising and delicate. "It could be mutually beneficial, Karina. You soothe my hunger, and I'll soothe yours."

"*Or* I could knee you in the balls again," I returned breathily, his presence heady and powerful.

Part of me wanted to throw all my human sensibilities out the window and kiss him soundly, but I was nowhere near brave enough to do it.

"You won't catch me off guard twice," he warned, his voice a delicious murmur as he pulled away from my throat. "No matter how clever or brave you are."

That snapped me out of the haze more than anything, surprise making me frown. He thought I was clever and brave? If only I had something equally complimentary to think of him. Instead, I thought he was suave and entitled and lethal.

His warm fingers caught my chin, tilting my face up, and I forgot to look away. He ensnared me in his gaze, and a deep clang of warning went through my soul at the eye contact.

"Remember what happened when you were remade," he ordered in a deep, hypnotic voice. "Remember what you've forgotten about your sire."

I didn't even blink, could do nothing but stare deep into crimson eyes, falling into them like I'd fallen into the river of blood in my dream.

The hazy image of my attacker sharpened into brutal clarity, and I inhaled sharply as memories battered me from every side. My head pounded. The teal and crimson bedroom wavered around me, even the scents shifting from fresh flowers and stale air to the rich paper and ink scent of the library and the coppery tang of blood.

"He killed my client," I said, my hands shaking. "I saw him dead, I tried to run..."

"And?" Lazarus pressed.

I couldn't see him in front of me anymore, but I could clearly picture the urgent demand on his face.

"Someone caught me; a man. He scratched me." I shuddered at the crystal clear image, the blond man was a psychopath through and through. But if he was Lorn, who was the man who'd scratched me?

I wavered, my knees weak, and Lazarus caught me around my waist.

"Alright," he said calmly. "Sit down, don't try to rush your memory."

My body met something soft and cushioned, presumably the bed, and I sat absentmindedly, my thoughts running fast, making connections in the pit of nothing that had existed there minutes ago.

"Who was the man who scratched you?" Lazarus asked, a strange contrast of impatient and gentle. I didn't trust it to last.

"I don't know," I muttered. "I've never met him before."

What if I couldn't lead Lazarus to Lorn? His progeny had to be the blond psychopath I remembered, the man who'd thrown me across a whole room into a bookshelf and left me broken there. The other man was his ... what? His minion? I strained my memory for his name, but all I got was a worse headache.

"If you ask too much of yourself too soon, you'll need more blood," Lazarus told me.

I gritted my teeth at the idea of feeding, letting memories rush at me like arrows, inhaling sharply as every one found its mark and pain flared.

"Show me," Lazarus said in a deeper voice, thrumming with compulsion.

I shuddered as warm fingers tilted my face up. I couldn't see him through my memories, the Witching Library as sharp as crystal around me, every window, bookcase, and leather spine as familiar as my own heartbeat.

The memories splintered apart when I remembered suddenly, cruelly, that I didn't have a heartbeat anymore.

Lazarus hissed, irritated. "Show me what happened," he commanded, and the memory reformed.

I gritted my teeth as the library snapped back into clarity in my mind. I could feel the softness of the bed underneath me, the mattress cradling my thighs, but around me the amber-lit library room blurred as I ran for my life, fear closing off my air.

"Show me your attacker," Lazarus murmured, his gravelly voice echoing through my memory.

Between one frantic breath and the next, I was on the threshold of the archives with a hand clamped around my throat and the blond psycho in front of me, speaking in a deceptively placid tone. Judging by Lazarus's hiss, I was right; this was Lorn.

He let go of me before he could see the other man, the one who'd scratched and threatened me.

I exhaled slowly, relief making me wobbly. If Lazarus never found out Lorn wasn't my sire, I'd be fine. If he realised the other man had turned me instead, what use would he have for me?

None, I knew.

I turned my phone over in my hands as the library faded, honestly surprised I was still holding it. I needed Lazarus; if I didn't know how to handle my hunger, I could never go home. Which meant he had to stay in the dark, and I had to keep a secret from a three-hundred year old vampire.

"Right," Lazarus said decisively, stepping away from me and flexing his hands. "Get some rest while you can. Tonight, we're going to the Witching Library."

"To do what?" I demanded, shaking away the memories —for now. I knew they'd return. They'd haunt me forever.

"I want to see where you were turned, and I want to know why Lorn was there to begin with."

My head throbbed as a memory tried to form, but all I saw was the archives room and my sire's leering face.

Lazarus wanted me to *go back* there? Tonight?

"I don't think—" I began, but when I glanced up Lazarus was gone, and I was alone in my new bedroom.

Get some rest? As if anything was that simple.

THIRTEEN

NATURALLY, I DIDN'T SLEEP. I LAID BACK ON THE luxurious bed, stifling a groan at how the soft mattress and velvet covers cradled my aching body, and stared at the whorls of plaster on the ceiling above me.

Eventually I called Mum, and then Aunt Jubilee, giving them the same story: *Ursula got me on a last minute conference and I think it'll be really good for me, so I'll be away for a few weeks.*

My ambitious, career-driven mum approved wholeheartedly, and made me promise to keep her updated with pictures of the 'hotel' where I was staying and the food I was eating. I'd have to figure out how to make that last part happen; maybe Lazarus would let me get a few snaps of Keith's dinner.

Aunt Jubilee was beside herself. Had I packed everything I needed for the trip? Had I remembered to take an extra pair of socks in case my feet got cold? My toothbrush was still in the holder in the bathroom; how would I survive without it? I hadn't even taken sandwiches for the journey, so I was—without a shadow of doubt—starving to death.

It took me a good twenty minutes to reassure my aunt I was fine, I wasn't hungry or cold or pining for my lost toothbrush. She only hung up when I promised to buy a brand new toothbrush. My skin was icy cold, my heart still, but I swore her fussing and care had warmed all my insides.

Ruby didn't reply to my text, but that wasn't unusual. The other text that came through with a low rumble of vibration made my heart figuratively stop. Ursula was furious that I hadn't turned up for work, especially given the library had been robbed and trashed and they needed all hands on deck setting it to rights.

"This is the last thing I need," I sighed, dragging my hands through my messy red hair. "First I lose my life, get kidnapped and forced into a bargain with an arrogant vampire, and now I might lose my damn job."

I wanted a book so badly, needed to vanish into make-believe worlds for a few hours.

Instead, I laid there and stared into space, letting my mind spin through everything that had happened, every memory that had returned to me—and everything about Lazarus Kaine that infuriated me. I began mentally listing things:

1. His devious smirk.
2. The way his eyes darkened when he'd backed me against the bureau.
3. His smug, confident air, like no one had ever denied him a single thing in his life.
4. The heartless way he'd bound me into helping him find Lorn.
5. The fact he was powerful enough to compel me into doing anything without my permission.
6. The way his touch burned.

7. He thought I was clever and brave.

Mostly, it pissed me off that he'd made me *want* him, when all I should want was to stab him in the back and run far away from here. I couldn't do that as long as I needed him, and the danger was I might end up enjoying the time I spent here.

Gnashing my sharp fangs, I shoved off the bed and explored the rest of my room, jumping when the TV turned on at a blaring volume and frantically fumbling for the remote. I pressed the volume down button so hard that the remote shattered.

"Shit," I hissed, shards of plastic and rubber buttons falling through my fingers to the carpet. My hearing was so acute I heard them bounce before settling at my feet.

I hastily picked up the broken pieces and hid them in a drawer, padding into the bathroom and relieved when there was nothing for me to break here, just a marble tub, sink, and toilet, all accented with warm brass. I had a lot of negatives about Lazarus, but his house was beautiful. At least I'd be comfortable while I learned how to be a non-killer vampire.

When I ran out of things to explore in my room, I hesitantly ventured into the rest of the house, exploring various guest rooms—including a suite entirely for Keith, furnished in the richest, most expensive materials—a dining room with a table empty of place settings, multiple receiving rooms in styles ranging from antique rose to gentleman's club to pure vampire ambience.

"Oh," I murmured when I turned a corner and found Keith sitting in the middle of the hallway. One grey leg was held above the plump cat's head like a dancer doing warm-up stretches, and his tongue frantically lapped somewhere indelicate.

He froze in the act to give me a baleful perusal, and found me severely lacking. I sighed, but I wasn't too disappointed; I knew it was the nature of cats to scorn new people.

"Hello, Keith," I greeted politely, watching as he lowered his leg in slow-mo, staring me out with bright yellow slit-pupiled eyes. "How's it going?"

He didn't lower himself to a reply; instead he climbed to his feet and turned his back on me, stalking away as if I'd highly disappointed him.

"He doesn't like you," a gravelly voice commented, and I jumped, spinning around with a hiss.

"Oh, it's you," I breathed, my shoulders sagging at the sight of Lazarus leaning in a doorway to my right, unexpectedly casual in a long-sleeved shirt rolled up to the elbows and dark-wash jeans, his long black hair falling loose around his shoulders. The three buttons at his collar were undone, offering a glimpse of pale skin and angular collarbones, and I suddenly became a Victorian gentleman obsessed by a tiny gleam of skin.

Gods dammit, I mentally snapped, dragging my stare away. I couldn't allow myself to become distracted; I needed to keep a clear head, or he'd discover Lorn wasn't really my sire.

Lazarus gazed down the hallway after his cat, a contemplative look on his face. "I've always trusted his opinion. He's an impeccable judge of character."

Oh, great. I suppressed a groan. "So now you don't trust me because your cat doesn't like me?"

"Exactly," Lazarus confirmed with a flash of a grin. "Better get started on winning him around. But not now; the sun's almost set, and I want to be out of the house the second it's dark."

"Wait," I blurted when he went back into the room he'd come out of. "I thought you were going to teach me how to control my hunger before we went out."

"Consider tonight your first lesson. If you get through the whole night without trying to eat anyone, you've passed."

"You're joking," I said flatly, watching through the open door as he hunted for a hair tie on a cluttered table, tying his hair into a messy ponytail. "Lazarus. You're joking right?"

He just snorted.

So not only did I need to find some clue to Lorn's whereabouts at the library, I also had to find a way not to attack anyone there.

"This is *not* going to end well," I muttered.

FOURTEEN

EVEN THOUGH IT WAS NIGHT, EVERY MUSCLE IN MY body tensed when I took my first step outside. I reminded myself I'd walked home last night, *and* walked along the river, but that was before the reality that I was undead had finally sunk in.

Now, there was no denying it. I hadn't eaten in twenty-four hours and I should have been starving, but I wasn't. I moved too fast, too gracefully, and with too much strength to be human. And the most damning evidence: my heart didn't beat.

If Lazarus noticed my pause, he didn't mention it. He just set off towards the tall, scrolling iron gates at the end of a short path. I peered over my shoulder at his house, not shocked to find a massive two-storey manor house, but pleasantly surprised that it was made of pale stone with ivy crawling up its surface. Less vampire-ish than its interior.

"We're still in London," I remarked, following him out the gates to a riverside walkway—the Thames walkway. "Where are we?"

I could see St. Pauls and the Shard, as well as the

towering glass structures of the City; we couldn't have been far from the centre.

"Southwark," he replied, holding the gate open for me and closing it behind us, an unreadable expression on his face. Was he waiting for me to run now I was out of his house? Was he planning how we'd trace Lorn's movements at the library? Was he already missing his cat? It was impossible to tell. "Not too far from Blackfriars Bridge."

"And you just have a house here?" I asked sceptically. "Right on the banks of the Thames."

No one had a house right on the banks of the Thames. Except, apparently, vampires.

Lazarus shrugged, his shoulders broad in a black wool coat. It suited him. "It's been in my family for generations."

"Your family...?" I pressed, inhaling cool river air as we walked deeper into the city. I knew next to nothing about Lazarus, and given he held my future in the palm of his annoyingly veiny hand, that was worrying. The more information I ferreted out about him, the better.

"My true family," he replied cagily, narrowing his eyes in my direction like he knew exactly why I was pushing. "That's all you need to know."

I exhaled a hard puff of air, shrugging. Fine, he didn't trust me. The feeling was mutual.

"Interesting how your true family don't live with you," I commented quietly, and knew he'd hear.

He stiffened with a little hiss, but I pretended not to hear as we walked past the Tate Modern, the Globe just ahead on our right, lit white against the dark sky. My stomach dropped at the sight of people milling around outside, bundled into thick coats and woollen hats to ward off the cold.

A ruthless hand closed around the back of my neck, and

I was actually relieved to feel fingernails bite into my skin, distracting pricks of pain drawing my attention to Lazarus.

"Lesson one," he said, keeping a close watch on me as the wind blew in our direction, carrying not the scent of coppery blood but something impossible to put into words. I needed it, needed it *right now*—

"You're always going to want to feed, so accept it," he continued in a low voice. "When you've accepted it, it's easier to fight."

My mouth watered, my fangs throbbing. With every step we took towards the Globe, my body strained to race across the small bit of space between me and the people, and I hated myself for it. Hated that I'd tasted blood, that I'd killed my neighbour, and I'd so readily do it again.

"It's better not to go somewhere densely populated, for obvious reasons. Are you listening, Karina?"

I swallowed against my dry throat, nodding absently, my gaze pinned on the humans. Or maybe some were supernaturals like us, seers like I used to be. It didn't matter; they were alive, and they called to me.

"Lesson two: you don't need to breathe."

I whipped my head around to Lazarus, sure I'd heard him wrong. "Excuse me?" I rasped, my voice like sandpaper.

"You don't need to breathe," he answered, serious and grave. He looked ready to march to war, not to teach a fledgling how to be a vampire. "So don't. If you don't breathe in the scent of their blood, it won't affect you."

I blinked, and blinked again. I didn't need to breathe. Okay. That was ... fine. And useful. "How do I...?"

"Just stop," he replied with a wry smile, digging his fingers into the back of my neck and pushing me past a particularly loud group of theatre-goers.

I dragged in a breath and struggled against his hold,

my muscles bunched and my stomach twisting into a knot. I couldn't smell the river anymore, or Lazarus's scent, only the divine, taunting scent of blood. But I mashed my lips shut and held the air in my lungs, straining against the urge to exhale and take another breath.

"Relax your shoulders," Lazarus coached, pressing his hand lower, into the knot between my shoulder blades. "You're not going to suffocate."

It *felt* like I was, like I'd die if I didn't drag another breath into my lungs.

The lights dancing on the black river blurred in my vision, but my lungs stopped burning and the suffocating sensation lessened, all my focus moving to the heat of Lazarus's hand on my back.

"Good," he praised flatly, and pushed me onward. "You'll need to breathe when you talk, but try to do it shallowly."

I nodded, fighting the natural instinct to breathe but able to do it without feeling like I would die. I didn't like a single second of it, but at least I kept my head as we passed the theatre. My fangs were swollen and pulsing, but at least I couldn't be tempted by blood.

I held my breath the rest of the way to the Witching Library, Lazarus walking close beside me, propelling me forward with a hand on my back. To any casual observer, we might have looked like a couple out for a night time stroll, rather than two people on the hunt for a murderer.

I took a slow sip of air as we scaled the wide, stone steps to the library, its many floors towering above us in an elegant scroll of arches, pillars, crystal-bright windows, and tan brick.

"Why does the council want to find my attacker so badly?" I asked, ducking through the heavy door Lazarus held open for me, a warning expression on his face as he glanced at me.

"You're smart enough to figure that out yourself," he replied, grabbing my arm as we stepped through the porch into the vast main room, the heart of the library. The place where I'd died.

"The attacks in the East End," I murmured, taking a shallow breath. "The humans have started speculating about a serial killer."

Lazarus nodded, surveying the library. "All attention is bad attention when we could be exposed."

My gaze shot right past the welcome desk and the many walnut bookcases and study desks, finding the spot where I'd crashed to the floor, helpless as venom spread to my heart.

"Karina," Lazarus warned, his voice dangerously low. His hand tightened around my arm, pressing through the fabric of my coat—which I'd found hung up in his closet, waiting for me.

I swallowed and pulled air into my lungs, trapping it there. I could think better when I couldn't smell the tempting scents around me, when the only taste on my tongue was old paper and crumbling ink.

"Show me where you saw Lorn," Lazarus ordered, keeping a stern eye on everyone in the room with us, as if the librarians and people checking out battered fiction books were going to draw knives and attack.

I nodded, not breathing as I ducked my head and led Lazarus through the murmur of rustling pages and low voices, the occasional squeak of a footstep coming from within the stacks at the edge of the room.

"Here," I whispered with what air I had left, pausing on the threshold between the main room and the west archives.

Cold dripped down my spine and I couldn't hold back the shudder as memories formed around me, startling in their clarity.

Cloves and honey stuffed up my nose, the bright red irises of Lorn's eyes took over my vision, and my ears were full of the deceptively friendly lull of his voice in the moment before he slammed his hand into my chest and sent me flying across the room. I flinched as, in my memory, I crashed into the bookshelf and fell to the floor, dazed and agonised.

"Karina," Lazarus said in a low voice, squeezing my arm.

I inhaled a jagged breath, blinking away the memory.

"This is where I saw him. There was another man with him," I added, careful not to give away that he was my sire. "He was the one who caught me trying to run."

Lazarus was quiet for a beat too long, drawing my attention to his clenched jaw and the dark glint in his eye as he looked at the destruction the archives had become. Someone had done a fair job of rescuing the most valuable books, but others were still strewn on the floor, and the heavy bookcases themselves were a toppled mess, solid wood cracked in places.

"You tried to run," Lazarus echoed, taking a step into the room and ushering me with him, so close to my side that soft warmth rippled from his body to thaw mine.

I laughed bitterly. "I didn't get far." I nodded at the end of the room, where the bookcases were collapsed on each other. "He threw me into that. Lorn. I hit it so hard that all this happened."

I jerked my arms at the destruction, ignoring the tight knot in my stomach. I was going to be sick, but the last thing I wanted to do was add vomit to the list of damages I'd done to my treasured archive.

Lazarus's head snapped to mine, his eyes sweeping my body.

"I'd have died without the scratch," I said, my voice strangely dull. I couldn't take my eyes off the crack in the bookcase where I'd hit. "I don't know if that means I should be grateful."

Lazarus just squeezed my arm again and nudged me deeper into the room, subtly placing himself between me and the door in case I was tempted to race back into the main room and eat someone. Another rush of cold moved through me at the idea of that, but that was the only word for it—*eat* someone. I was a vampire, and that was what vampires did. We ate, we drank, and we killed.

I'd done all three in the last two days alone.

Was this better than being dead? I stared at the crack in the bookcase, and wasn't sure.

A low whistle from behind made me jump, and I cut off my air supply, grabbing the hand Lazarus had on my arm like it was a life preserver in a storm.

Shit. *Ruby*.

My best friend leaned against the doorframe with a smirk on her light brown face and an eyebrow raised suggestively. A cloud of dark curls framed her face, the ends brushing her purple leather jacket.

"Here I was worrying about you when you didn't show for work, and you've sloped off with a handsome man." Her brown eyes glittered in her heart-shaped face. "I'm proud, Karina, honestly."

"Who is this?" Lazarus asked mildly, but his grip was bruising on my arm and his body had tensed in threat and warning. I had to get Ruby out of here ASAP.

"Ruby Omir," my best friend replied, giving him a judging once-over. "Her bestie. The bestie you'll have to answer to if you upset her. And just so you know, I might look cute and cuddly, but I know Krav Maga."

Lazarus exhaled a laugh through his nose, the corner of his mouth curling up. "Which you just announced to me. Not very smart of you, Ruby."

Ruby shot me a look. "He's a dick, Karina."

"I know." I shrugged, trying to look casual while I took the smallest breath. My stomach cramped instantly as a scent hit me—Ruby's scent. My fangs throbbed painfully, my mouth watering. "But it's not like that. I'm working with him."

Ruby gave me a sceptical look, but the tightness of my expression probably looked nothing like the glow of a new relationship, *or* the rush of a hook-up. "We should go out some time soon," she said, watching me. "Do you want to see a film?"

My chest tightened. Our secret code—all I needed to do for Ruby to help me was agree that we should go to the cinema. All I had to say was yes, one little word. But tonight was proof that I couldn't control myself, even with cutting off my breathing. I couldn't be trusted around my mortal friends.

"Not this week," I replied, my throat tight. "Maybe some other time?"

Ruby relaxed, a relieved smile brightening her face. "Definitely. I'm watching you—guy," she finished, realising Lazarus hadn't offered his name. "You take care of my girl, or I'm coming for your balls with a chainsaw."

A laugh burst out of me, using up the last of my air. But it felt good to laugh, felt good to release my nerves in a rush of sound. It had only been a day, but I missed Ruby like hell.

"Alright, well I'll leave you to your work," Ruby said,

tucking her hands in the pocket of her violet jacket. "What-ever that mysterious work *is*. Text me later," she added, fixing me with a stare. I prayed she didn't notice the stillness of my chest. "I've got a date tomorrow, and I need your help picking a dress."

I nodded, taking the smallest breath and fighting a shudder at the scent that slid across my taste buds, filling my mouth with saliva. "I will," I promised, trembling in Lazarus's hold. His hand was like iron around my arm, and I was so glad of it.

Horror nearly made me sick when Ruby started towards me, her arms opening for a hug. I could kill her. I could really, honestly kill her, and it would take me *a second* to rip out her throat.

I opened my mouth to warn her, to make some excuse, to beg her to stay away—anything—but a shadow fell across the doorway and a horribly welcome voice said, "*Ruby.* Shouldn't you be reshelving on the mezzanine? That is, after all, what I pay you for."

Ruby's face shuttered, smoothing to a neutral, respectful expression. "Sure, Ursula, I was just leaving."

My stomach writhed like a pit of snakes. Was I even allowed to be here? Ursula had sent me a warning, and it was my room that was wrecked, after all. Maybe she'd throw me out.

We hadn't found any clue to Lorn's whereabouts, and hadn't unlocked any more memories. We couldn't leave the library yet.

Ruby slipped past Ursula's tall, imposing frame—she reminded me of a praying mantis, all elegance and murderous grace—and made a wincing face behind our boss's back.

I gulped. Even if I hadn't been cutting off my air, I

doubted I'd be able to breathe as Ursula settled the full weight of her disapproving gaze upon me.

No one knew exactly what species Ursula was, or even which order she belonged to. Some said she was a dark witch, others an elf or angel, but Ruby and I swore she was a gargoyle. She might have no wings, but she was freezing cold stone alright.

"Where have you been?" Ursula demanded in a chilling tone that made me swallow hard.

"I..."

Lazarus gripped my arm harder and stepped in front of me, his voice shockingly deep and hypnotic when he spoke.

"Karina is helping me with a council matter of utmost urgency. She'll be unavailable for weeks, so find someone else to cover her job."

I peered around Lazarus's broad shoulder, jolting in surprise at the glassy look in Ursula's eyes. My boss was untouchable, wholly terrifying ... and Lazarus had compelled her like it was nothing.

"You'll tell no one else that she's helping the council. If anyone asks, she's on holiday—"

"At a conference," I put in hastily.

"At a conference," he corrected, his voice deeper, resonant in a way that made my skin buzz. "You won't come looking for Karina. Forget meeting me."

A memory shot through me like a javelin, and I stumbled.

Forget Keaton. Forget the codex. But remember me.

"Go," Lazarus commanded, his voice dripping with power and danger. He didn't even watch to make sure Ursula obeyed his command before he turned to me.

My breath caught at the violence in his dark red eyes, at the terrifying expression making his face gaunt and monstrous. For the first time I was really, truly afraid of Lazarus, and painfully aware of how fragile I was at his mercy.

"What is it?" he demanded, catching my shoulders in a gentle hold that jarred me. I'd been expecting bruises and brutality. "Shit, you're shaking."

I wet my lips, inhaling through my nose and shaking when the scents from the main room hit my senses—along with the lingering aroma of lifeblood in this room. My best friend's and my boss's. Given half a chance, I'd attack them.

"There was a codex," I rasped, my throat shredded to ribbons as I swallowed. I strained against Lazarus's hold, my breathing coming faster, my fangs aching to sink into flesh and drain blood from a vital vein—

"Karina." Lazarus shook me, his eyes honed on my face. For a second, I thought he was going to kill me. Or kiss me. "A codex? What codex?"

I blinked slowly, my thoughts dragging sluggishly. My mouth filled with saliva, my lungs full of the scent of blood. I could smell my own, the lingering traces where my scratch had welled and blood had dropped on the wooden boards in this room and the next. Heartbeats thudded all around me, filling the library, tempting me—

The hands tightened on my shoulders as I tried to race towards that sweet, delicious scent.

"What happened just now?" the vampire restraining me demanded, hauling me deeper into the wreckage of the archives. "You were under control one second, and feral the next. Tell me about the codex, Karina."

I bared my fangs and hissed, senseless with need.

He held me with one hand—so strong I couldn't escape even that grip—and reached into the pocket of his coat, pulling out a plastic pouch full of dark red liquid.

When he pressed it to my mouth, I hissed in the back of my throat. But when the smell of blood reached my nose through the plastic, I sliced through it with my fangs and groaned at the first taste.

I couldn't smell anything but the rich sweetness of the blood, like honey and syrup on my senses, couldn't taste anything but the ambrosia sliding down my throat. I squeezed the pouch until it was empty, sucking out every last drop and shuddering in relief.

When I blinked and refocused on my surroundings, we were hidden by a fallen bookcase, shielded in a pocket of darkness while I fed like a ravenous beast.

"Oh gods," I breathed, reeling and sick. "I can't—I can't do this."

Lazarus took the empty pouch from me before I could throw it away in horror, tucking it out of sight in his coat. I froze when he grabbed my chin, forcing me to meet his stare.

"No one died. You controlled yourself admirably at first. And I was here to keep you in check the whole time. How do you feel now?"

"Sick," I whispered, my face tingling and hot as tears built in my eyes. I didn't want to cry in front of him, but I couldn't help it.

"The first few weeks are rough," he admitted, holding my gaze with a mixture of ruthlessness and understanding. "You did well tonight."

I shook my head. If he hadn't been holding me, I'd have slaughtered my way through the library—and that was *doing well?*

"What did you remember?" he prompted, tilting his dark head to the side as he watched me with intent eyes. "You said there was a codex."

I swallowed, the taste of blood lingering in my mouth. My head shot through with pain, but the memory was there —faded, but coming through.

"Someone had requested the Codex of Fiends from the archives. It's an encyclopaedia, ancient, hardly ever checked out."

"What happened?" Lazarus pressed, keeping my gaze captive as he searched my face.

"I saw him dead." At his frown, I swallowed and explained, "I can see the future, usually in fractured visions. Or at least I could before I was killed. Now ... I don't know. I haven't tried." I was too afraid to. "That was when I ran, and when the vampires found me."

Lazarus's mouth thinned. "Show me the other man."

He lifted his hand to my forehead, and I inhaled sharply, scrambling for a safe memory I could show him that wouldn't reveal my secret.

Ignoring how much it chilled me, I remembered when my sire held my throat in the doorway, remembered the glimpse I'd got of him before Lorn threw me across the room: dark hair, intense eyes, and cruelty in his smile.

Lazarus hissed, a menacing sound that sent freezing cold down my spine.

"Keaton," he said in a voice as cold as a glacier, letting go of me to put space between us.

"You know him?" I realised.

I buried my shaking hands in the pockets of my coat, dragging in the familiar book-scented air to calm myself. I'd missed the library, my second home, but being back here felt strange. Like walking into your childhood home and finding the furniture rearranged and décor all new.

"He's Lorn's right hand man," Lazarus replied, flexing his pale hands in and out of fists. There was a silvery scar across the back of his left hand, a ragged slash that must have hurt like hell if it had scarred even his vampire body. "And I know just where to find him. Come on, Karina."

I jolted when he turned and left the dark shelter of our little nook.

With no other choice, I hurried after him, suddenly breathless at the thought of being alone. How many people would I kill if Lazarus wasn't here to keep me in check?

"Where are we going?" I asked, breathing as little as possible as Lazarus stalked into the main room of the Witching Library, ignoring everyone studying at the tables in the central aisle. He paused, just slightly, when we passed the place my heart had taken its last beat, as if he could scent my blood.

"To see Keaton," he replied in a dark tone.

My stomach shot down to the floor. I couldn't let him speak to Keaton—he'd find out Lorn wasn't my sire, and then he'd get rid of me. And after tonight, it was clearer than ever that I needed to stay with Lazarus.

"Problem?" Lazarus asked, turning to me with a raised eyebrow when he noticed I was dragging my feet.

"No," I replied hastily. "No problem."

He narrowed his eyes like he didn't quite believe me. I held my breath as we passed through the rest of the library and onto the lamplit street, feeling like my new life was a fragile house of cards about to fall down around me.

FIFTEEN

Blood beaded as I bit my lip, anxiety a sickness in my stomach. I couldn't think of a single reason why we shouldn't follow this lead to Lorn's henchman. It should be a positive thing, a direction to follow when we'd had none. I came up with a dozen different potential reasons as we took a series of back alleys and side streets around London Bridge, and dismissed every single one.

Lazarus wasn't an idiot; he'd see straight through my lies.

"What if this Keaton doesn't even know anything?" I tried finally, my stomach twisting into a pretzel of fear.

Something thumped in my chest—not my heart, but something scarily similar to a heartbeat. Was this the bond Lazarus mentioned between sire and progeny? Was my sire —Keaton—close by?

"He's just a henchman, right?" I went on. "I doubt Lorn tells him all his plans."

"I don't need to know Lorn's plans," Lazarus answered grimly, focused on the hunt as he stalked through a puddle reflecting the moon above, the tiny alleyway empty except for us. "I just need to find him, bind him, and hand him to the council."

"Why?" I asked, hoping to distract him but also curious. I wrapped my coat tighter around myself—not because I felt the chill, but because it was all the reassurance and protection I had. "Why is it so important?"

"You already figured that out," he replied dismissively. "Lorn has a hand in the attacks in Wapping and Greenwich."

"No." I shook my head, wincing at a distant shout from rowdy pub-goers. My ears picked up every sound, little or loud, and no matter how hard I tried to shut them out, they stabbed my head like needles. "Not why does the council want them. Why do *you* want to hand him over so badly? Are you in trouble with the council?"

The look Lazarus shot me was as cold and brutal as stone, and I shuddered. It occurred to me that Lazarus might be wanted by the council himself, and not actually a councilman as he'd told me. Maybe he was trying to barter for his own freedom. Maybe he was a mass murderer.

He bared his teeth with a hiss, clearly reading everything on my face. I'd never been good at concealing my emotions.

"I need the council on side, and finding Lorn will impress them. That's all you need to know."

A dozen dark theories flitted through my mind, but Lazarus wouldn't hurt me as long as I helped him. And at least I could run fast if he turned out to be a madman.

I nodded silently, cutting off my breathing when the bawdy shouts grew louder, closer.

"Good," Lazarus praised, as if we didn't both know I thought he was an axe murderer. "You're learning."

I was silent, scrambling for a way to stop this meeting.

Rain began to speckle the cobbles, slicing past the collar of my coat to drip down my spine. I should have slid on the wet stones, but vampire grace kept me on my feet without even a wobble.

I resented it—my new body, my new senses, my new abilities. I just wanted to go back to my regular mortal body, with all its flaws. I wanted my old life back.

"In here," Lazarus said abruptly, and I startled when he pushed open the door of a small, leaning pub on the corner of the alleyway and a back street. A Meatloaf song thumped inside, rattling the warped, multi-coloured windows and my eardrums.

I ground to a halt before the solid step into the inn, the middle of the stone worn down by hundreds upon hundreds of feet. I could imagine the tantalising scent of blood from within, and was glad I wasn't breathing.

"Keaton owns this pub," Lazarus explained, watching me with one hand holding the door open. "Come on, I'll buy you a drink."

I nearly groaned. I needed a drink as badly as I wanted blood, but the last thing I wanted was to go inside a pub owned by my sire. I shook my head, my jaw clenched.

"Inside," Lazarus ordered, his crimson eyes narrowed. "You'll be fine, Karina, just don't breathe."

I bit my bottom lip. He thought it was fear of being in such a small space that held me back. Maybe it was better that he did think that.

I shook my head, backing up three steps, fear making my hands shake and prickle.

"Karina," Lazarus growled, his voice deeper, fuller. "Unless you want the council's shadowhounds to tear you apart in three weeks, get in the damn pub."

The compulsion he wrapped around the last five words made me stiffen, and I bared my teeth even as my feet dragged me up the warped step, past Lazarus's tense body, and into the small, cloying room on the other side of the pub.

SIXTEEN

I DIDN'T BREATHE, DIDN'T DARE MOVE surrounded by so many mortals, but I couldn't stop shaking as Lazarus gestured for me to sit on a stool at the bar that had seen many better days.

The pub wasn't full by any means, but my hearing was overwhelmed by a couple dozen voices talking over each other, shifting in their seats, and chairs squeaking as they were pushed back. Even without my sense of smell, I was painfully aware of the warmth and motion of every single person.

I jumped at the loud clunk of a wine bottle meeting the solid wood in front of me, and I frowned at Lazarus, not daring to breathe enough to ask what the hell he was playing at.

"I told you I'd buy you a drink," he reminded me, slanting a look in my direction as he took the seat beside me.

My shoulders were up by my ears as I scanned the pub for Keaton, my skin crawling all over. I grabbed the bottle and took long gulps, downing a third of it in one go.

Lazarus blinked, looking both concerned and impressed. "If you finish the bottle, you might feel a little buzz. Takes a lot to get a vampire drunk," he added in a low voice, so the humans oblivious to supernaturals didn't overhear. "But since you're so new, you can probably get tipsy on a bottle."

I wanted to ask how much alcohol it took to get *him* drunk, but I didn't dare speak, so I just tipped the bottle back and ignored the judging stares aimed my way as I swallowed gulp after gulp. I'd come a long way from the librarian seer who couldn't drink three glasses and walk in a straight line.

"Hain," Lazarus said, waving over a thirty-something man with messy blond hair and a scar through his lip. His nose was bumpy, as if it had been broken more than once, and the scowl on his face gave the impression of someone unafraid to get into a fight if someone pissed him off.

"What?" he barked at Lazarus, grabbing three empty glasses and stowing them beneath the bar.

My hands shook around the wine bottle, and I drank more for liquid courage. Who was this Hain? Did he know Keaton? He must have done if he worked in his pub, right? Would he take one look at me and know, somehow, that I was Keaton's progeny?

"I'm looking for Keaton. Or Lorn," Lazarus said, leaning forward with a narrowed glare.

Hain snorted, grabbing a clean glass and pulling a pint. "You've got a death wish, Lazarus. I know he's your kid, but I'd stay clear away. I haven't seen him, and I hope I never do."

"Why?" Lazarus asked, all his attention honed on the barman.

Hain set the pint on the bar and began another, not

even looking at Lazarus. "He's a psycho. And that's coming from me."

I shuddered, Lorn's mild smile and friendly expression fixed in my memory now it had been returned to me. I'd seen the true Lorn in the split second before he'd thrown me across the archives, his mask falling away to reveal the predator within.

"What if I made it worth your while?" Lazarus asked, watching Hain like a hawk watched a mouse.

Hain's stare flicked up to Lazarus, and then back to the pint, setting it on the bar when it had a perfect, foamy head. I could hear the quickening thump of his heartbeat, and my mouth watered even if I couldn't smell the blood in his body. I didn't know what species he was, but he certainly wasn't undead. My stomach cramped despite the blood still sloshing in it; I drowned it with more wine, my hands shaking harder.

While I was distracted, Lazarus slid a fifty pound note across the bar; with a swift grin, Hain pocketed it and said, "Speak to Thatcher. That lad over there. He's been on a few jobs with Keaton from what I've heard. If anyone knows where to find your psycho son, it's him."

"Thanks," Lazarus said, still in his dark, scary tone. He gave me a look that very clearly ordered me to stay put, but I was too nervous of what Thatcher might tell him—whoever Thatcher even was—that I slid off my stool and followed him.

I was surprised at how my head spun. It was the most human I'd felt since becoming a vampire.

With how closely danger pressed against me here, it wasn't a good feeling. I needed to be in full control to make sure my secret stayed secret.

"Which one of you is Thatcher?" Lazarus asked, casually approaching the table Hain had pointed out.

A scrawny man who couldn't have been more than nineteen shot out of his seat, the blood draining from his face as he threw the chair over and ran. A thumping sense in my chest told me he was a vampire, and a deep, prickling sensation ran down my arms.

"Go out the front," Lazarus barked at me, his expression as dark as a storm.

Eager to catch Thatcher first, I scrambled for the exit, my body responding eagerly to the command to run.

I barely processed the rickety tables and well-loved chairs I raced past at vampire speed, was barely conscious of the heavy door I pushed open like it was made of cardboard. Two days ago, I'd have struggled with the weight, but now it was nothing.

With my half-empty wine bottle in hand, I exploded into the drizzling night, pricking my ears for the soft scrape of footsteps—coming in my direction.

My breath caught, and I trapped it in my chest lest any unsuspecting humans come this way. The last thing I needed right now was for the irresistible scent of honeyed blood to distract me from Thatcher.

I needed to know what he knew. Innocent people didn't run; he knew *something*. I just hoped it had nothing to do with me.

I tilted my head as I listened to the vampire get closer, and I was vaguely conscious of the fact it was Lazarus's gesture I'd mirrored.

The footsteps neared, too quiet for human ears to pick up but scraping the cobbles loud enough for me to place Thatcher at four steps away. And then three. And then two, the rustling of his puffy jacket audible as a plastic-y crackling. And then one, the vampire hissing swear words under his breath.

I trusted my hearing and my new speed, not waiting for visual confirmation before I swung my arm with all my might. The wine bottle shattered upon impact with Thatcher's dirty blonde head, and he was sent sprawling to the ground, more from shock than injury.

It was enough time for me to jump on him, for my knee on his chest to pin him to the slick cobblestones. He had to be older than me, which meant he could overpower me, but right now I had the edge and I was going to take full advantage of it.

If I'd been alive, my heart would have been pounding, sweat beading at my temples to give away my nerves. I felt like a fraud, like he'd know I was terrified rather than terrifying, but I pulled on a mask, emulating every badass book character I'd ever read.

I was Elizabeth Bennet, facing down Lady Catherine De Burgh. I was Eowyn defying orders to kill the Witch-King of Angmar. I was Katniss, shattering the Capitol with a handful of berries.

"Tell me what you know," I demanded in a voice I'd never heard from myself before. I wasn't the introverted librarian or the anxious artist right now. I was a vampire—dangerous and unpredictable.

"Nothing," Thatcher swore, his voice reedy and afraid. I pretended he was scared of me rather than Lazarus, stalking lazily towards us. "Nothing, I swear. I swear."

"I don't believe you," I replied coldly, grabbing his shoulder and slamming him into the ground. A sick fizzle of satisfaction went through my belly, almost like butterflies, and exhilaration made me shivery. "You ran for a reason. Tell me."

"He'll kill me," Thatcher whined, his watery-red eyes wide and bloodshot. "You don't understand, he's not like the rest of us. I can't cross him."

"You can't cross me, either," I told him, tilting my head—intentionally this time—in a slow perusal, like I was deciding whether to keep him alive or not. I watched his throat bob, honestly surprised that had worked to spook him. "I could kill you, too."

He bucked, nearly sending me flying off him, but I dug my hands into his shoulders and set all my weight on the knee I'd braced on his chest. I was enjoying this, I realised, and wondered what the hell was wrong with me. I didn't do daring things like this. I didn't go around throwing people to the floor.

It felt good, though. There was no denying that.

"I used to work for him, okay?" Thatcher breathed, his wide eyes fixed on me as I stared down at him. "He's always been controlling and scary as hell, but ever since the last blood moon, he's something else. He knows everything, sees everything. He's more powerful than I've seen him before, and no way in *hell* am I telling you anything."

"You already have," Lazarus drawled, stopping his dangerous prowl a few feet away. I could sense his eyes on me, a not-unpleasant weight, but I kept my focus on Thatcher as the reedy vampire squirmed. "Where is he hiding?"

Thatcher burst out laughing, his body shaking with it, and unease curled through me. "Hiding? If you think he's hiding, you're insane. He's busy—there's a difference. I don't know what he's planning, and I wouldn't tell you if I did."

"Where is he?" Lazarus demanded in a scary-calm voice, his shadow falling over us as he stepped closer.

"I don't fucking know!" Thatcher shouted, loud enough to make my ears fuzzy.

I hissed, gnashing my teeth, and pressed my knee harder into his chest.

"Fine." Lazarus shrugged. "Kill him."

A bolt of alarm went through me—but it wasn't a command, wasn't wrapped in his compulsion. I could refuse. No way was I going to actually, consciously *kill* someone.

But Thatcher didn't know that, and he was too dizzy with fear to notice the shock on my face.

"Please!" he begged. "Please, don't. I've told you everything I know. That's it, that's all I know. I haven't seen him in weeks, he's busy working on something he doesn't need me for, and he's scary as fuck. He ripped out Vohan's throat with his teeth the last time I saw him, and that bastard's as old as London itself."

I glanced at Lazarus, judging his opinion. I believed the whiny vampire pinned to the ground beneath me. He was so scared, he'd have confessed anything to save his life. If he knew anything, he'd have told us.

And if he'd have known about Lorn not being my sire, he'd have said that, too. A knot eased in my chest, and I leaned my weight off Thatcher.

"If you see Lorn," Lazarus said, his tone still dark and dreadful, "tell him I have a proposition for him."

I saw Lazarus nod to me from the corner of my eye, and I moved away, getting clumsily to my feet. Muscles protested at being stretched in ways they were unused to— even my vampire body had limits, it seemed—but I found my balance fast enough to watch Thatcher scramble upright and race away, not questioning his good luck.

"A proposition?" I asked Lazarus, leaning against the

side of the pub and breathing fast. Exhilaration raced through my blood, and my hunger had dimmed. Lazarus was right; violence did help. It was a worrying discovery.

Lazarus shrugged, staring down the narrow road as if he could see where Thatcher had run to. "There isn't one, but Lorn is greedy and egotistical enough to think he can out-scheme me. Probably to think he can kill me in the process."

"You don't get along then?" I asked dryly, waiting for my breathing to slow and listening for the creak of the pub door, ready to cut off my breathing if a mortal came out.

"Not in the least," Lazarus agreed, coming closer. "You did well tonight. How do you feel?"

I shrugged. Alive, afraid of what it meant to feel so alive by threatening someone, a little amazed at myself. Mostly stunned at the whole thing.

"I'm fine," I replied, breaking eye contact.

But the reality of what we'd found from Thatcher settled heavily around me: nothing. Nothing at all.

"Finding Lorn is impossible," I muttered, stalking down the street away from the pub. Lazarus followed, watching me so closely my face prickled. "We have no idea where to start, no idea why he killed me, or if he's going to kill anyone else. Nothing to convince the shadowhounds to leave me alive."

The more I spoke, the faster I breathed, the more my frustration and fear grew.

"What was the point of coming here? We were supposed to find something to lead us to Lorn, so you could take him to the council, and I could go fucking *home!*"

I walked faster with every step, stomping through puddles on the cobblestones. My hands shook, and all my adrenaline shifted from the high of violence to fury at what I'd become. Streets blurred fast, my feet barely whispering over the old stones. Lazarus stalked me like a shadow.

"I shouldn't even be here!" I shouted, spinning to pin him with a glare.

He stopped a few feet away, watching me with a dangerous calm. He took his hands out of his coat pockets, keeping them ready to grab me.

"I should be at home, worrying about the extra work Ursula had just dumped on me, not here, interrogating a vampire!"

"I know," Lazarus agreed calmly.

I bared my teeth, a hiss in the back of my throat. I wanted to attack him, but I knew that was crazy. I wanted—I wanted to run. To go home.

I tensed my muscles, twisting into a run—and slammed into a hard, muscular back with enough force to rattle my brain.

"I don't think so, baby vamp."

My head spun. How had he got here so fast? Why was I upside down, all the blood rushing to my head?

"Let me go!" I hissed, deep and throaty. The wool of his coat scratched my cheek as he set off walking, his steps brisk. "If you don't let me go, I'll—"

Well, I didn't know what I'd do. The woman who'd threatened Thatcher was gone, replaced by resentment and homesickness, and I didn't have any clever threats to wield against him. Not that Lazarus would be as easy to intimidate as Thatcher had been.

"Go on," he taunted, silky with amusement. "I'm dying to know what you'll do to me."

"No," I replied, struggling against his hold. His hands were clamped around the backs of my thighs, my head bouncing off his back as he walked. He carried me like a sack of damn potatoes, and I was spitting mad about it. Literally—spitting and hissing like a cat in a bath. "Then you'll know what to expect."

"Clever," he praised, but heavy on condescension.

"What are you going to do with me?" I demanded, and it was as if the past twelve hours hadn't happened. We hadn't struck a bargain, he hadn't given me my own room to stay in while I figured out how to be a good vampire, we hadn't developed a fragile camaraderie at the Witching Library. No, again I was his captured quarry.

"Throw you in the river," he replied dryly, and then snorted when I bristled. "You're coming back home with me, and we're going to work off all your aggression."

I opened my mouth, a protest on the tip of my tongue.

"No arguments," he cut me off with a scary, dark tone. "Unless you'd rather stay out here, unsupervised, and become as hunted as your sire."

I hissed, but I had no choice but to stop fighting and accept that Lazarus wasn't letting go of me until I was locked up in his home again.

SEVENTEEN

"CHOOSE A WEAPON," LAZARUS SAID WITH A magnanimous sweep of his hand at the massive training room in his manor house.

He ignored that I was glaring daggers at him, my fangs bared on a deep hiss.

"I'd advise against a broadsword, since you don't have the strength for it yet, but if you want to make a fool of yourself, go right ahead."

I watched him cross the polished wood floor in the direction of a small collection of wooden staffs, and my temper just *snapped*. I needed an outlet for all my fear, all my hatred of my hunger and my body, and for all my frustration that we'd never find Lorn, that I'd never get to go back to my old life. Lazarus just happened to represent every single aspect.

I was across the room in a heartbeat, my shoes not even squeaking on the floorboards as I cut through the air, my breath ragged and fast.

Lazarus's rumbling laugh wasn't a good sign, especially when it continued even when I launched at his back and wrapped my hands around his throat. I didn't want to kill him, I didn't even want to hurt him—it wasn't his fault I was a vampire, but it was certainly thanks to him that I hadn't killed anyone tonight—but I had too much energy brimming inside me, and it transmuted into violence.

"No weapons, then," he remarked, unwrapping my hands from around his neck and dropping me to my feet on the floor. "As you wish, baby vamp."

"Stop calling me that," I bit out, adjusting my weight on my feet and watching him turn slowly, assessing my stance. I knew it must be all wrong; I was hardly used to throwing punches in my day job. "It's irritating."

"But you *are* a vampire, and you're a baby," he pointed out, an infuriating little smirk in the corner of his mouth. He rolled up the sleeves of his silky shirt, unfastening the top three buttons, and it was suddenly hard to focus. "Come on, then," he taunted. "If you really want to take your anger out on me, try to hit me."

I curled my hands into fists, but hesitated. Did I really want to get into a fight with a three-hundred-year-old vampire I didn't really know and definitely couldn't trust?

"Unless you don't think you can," he added, tilting his head. "I understand if you're intimidated—"

My temper spiked even higher than before, and I swung my fist at his jaw, throwing all my body weight into the move like I'd read in a book. I threw a little *too much* weight into it, and spun alarmingly fast, losing my footing.

Lazarus caught me with my back to his chest, his arms like a cage around my waist. "Sloppy, Karina, very sloppy."

I snarled, wrenching away from him and surprised when he let me go. I faced him again, lifting my hands in front of my face and curling them into fists.

"You'll be sloppy by the time I'm finished with you," I threw back at him, startled when he laughed.

Lazarus crooked a finger at me, a little smile still on his face. Simmering, I feigned disinterest in hitting him again—and launched forward a second later, hoping to catch him off guard.

No chance. He caught my wrists instantly, trapping them in his long fingers, and I huffed in annoyance.

"What's the point in this if you won't let me hit you?"

Lazarus shrugged, running his thumb along the veins in one of my wrists before letting go. He did it to throw me off balance and it worked. I gritted my teeth, ignoring the prickles moving from my face down my neck in lieu of a blush.

"It's always good to have high aspirations," he purred. I wasn't sure if he was still trying to unsettle me or if he was genuinely flirting. "Think of how accomplished you'll feel when you finally hit me."

Next time, I didn't play around; I adjusted my balance and flew at him with as much speed as I could, hoping a kamikaze approach would work.

He caught my wrist two inches from his body, but it was the closest I'd got. My breathing was fast, my skin shivery with the thrill.

"Really?" Lazarus taunted. "That's the best you can do?"

I bared my teeth in a grin. I'd once told Ruby that librarians didn't do extreme sports, and climbing the rolling ladders in the Witching Library was as close as I'd come. This was a world apart, but I was starting to enjoy myself.

I didn't reply to Lazarus's taunt; I threw one fist at him, and then another, taking advantage of my speed and strength to attack him with a blur of punches. He blocked each one, but the smack of my fist into his palm was still satisfying, the ripple of impact up my arm exhilarating. My blood sparked, my breathing faster.

"Better," Lazarus said stoically, meeting my every hit with a lazy kind of grace. "You've got no skill, but at least you're using your speed."

I tried to use my speed to punch him in the stomach, but it was probably a good thing that he knocked my fist aside. Judging by the rest of him, his stomach would be as solid as a stone wall, and I'd end up with more than the bruised knuckles I had now.

"Clumsy," he remarked, raising an eyebrow. "Have you never thrown a punch before tonight?"

"No," I huffed, exasperated. "When would I ever need to hit someone? I don't know what things were like when *you* were alive, but normal people just don't go around punching people in the face."

Lazarus laughed quietly, watching me with sharp interest. "You talk like I was born in the iron age."

"Weren't you?" I fired back, assessing him for somewhere new to hit. Or to *try* to hit.

I feigned right—that was a thing, right? Feigning? I'd read it in a bunch of books—and flung my fist left, skimming his ribs with my knuckles before he batted my arm aside.

I'd hit him! Kinda. Feigning was my new favourite thing. I tried it again, but he evaded my hit faster this time, and I got a throbbing spot on my arm for the attempt.

"Keep going," Lazarus murmured, watching every move. "You'll hit me eventually. Even if we're still here tomorrow," he added with a smirk.

Smug bastard. I did exactly as he said, raining blows at his face, his chest, even aiming a knee very badly at his crotch. I kept waiting to tire, to run out of breath, but I didn't get so much as a stitch in my side as I threw punch after punch, every single one of them blocked.

This was useless. There was no way I could beat Lazarus in a fight, even in a training session; he was older, faster, stronger, and far more skilled. But I remembered all my favourite literary heroines, and wondered if I could beat him with cleverness instead.

I didn't even know why hitting him was so important, but my pride wouldn't let me back down after so much effort put into it now.

I let my fists drop and huffed a deep, growly sigh, a sulky expression on my face. It wasn't entirely faked, but I dialled it up as I shook my head and turned.

"Karina," Lazarus said.

I ignored him, my steps dragging across the shiny training room floor. "I've had enough," I muttered.

"Wow," he drawled. "Giving up so soon?"

"Yep," I replied caustically, smothering my smile at the sound of pursuing footsteps.

"Come on," he placated, catching my elbow. "A few more minutes. It's not good to walk away when you're so frustrated. I'll even let you get a hit in—"

I spun with all my vampire speed and fired my fist into his ribs, a solid hit against his side that shook up my arm and made my bruised knuckles flare with a deeper ache.

"No worries," I replied with a smile I didn't even try to stifle. A thrill went through my belly at the dark look on Lazarus's sculpted face—and an even deeper, far more dangerous thrill rippled through me when he grinned crookedly. "I don't need you to *let* me hit you. I'm doing just fine."

I was absolutely not, but the single hit had gone to my

head—and to my ego. Cocky, I crossed my arms over my chest and gave him a smug little smile.

"Now you're fighting like a vampire," he said, bemused and—unless I was imagining it—impressed.

"Does it hurt?" I asked, only half feigning concern. I wasn't used to hitting someone; I was more used to stressing over *accidentally* hurting someone. One time I'd been so piled with books that I'd walked into a junior librarian and bruised her cheek, and I'd never got over it.

Lazarus smirked, leaning closer. Enough for his earthy scent to overwhelm my senses. "I'll live. How do you feel?"

"Better," I admitted. "Who knew all I needed was to hit you?"

He snorted. "Don't get used to it. Now I know you fight like a trickster, I'll be waiting for it."

My throat bobbed when he brushed a strand of sweaty red hair off my cheek, and again I couldn't tell if he was flirting or trying to unsettle me.

"I'll just have to be more clever," I said, breathier than intended.

"Mm," he agreed, his red eyes dark as he watched me. If I'd had a pulse, it would have been racing. "You're just full of surprises, baby vamp."

I huffed, moving away with a scowl. "I told you not to call me that. It's annoying."

"I know," he replied, grin deepening until a dimple showed in his cheek. "That's why I'll keep calling you that. You're cute when you're angry."

I blinked, unaccustomed to compliments. Especially from insanely sexy, ageless vampires with messy black hair and sultry red eyes who looked far too good covered in a light sheen of sweat.

Oh dammit, I was in lust with him, wasn't I? This was *not* in the plan.

"You want me to hit you again so badly?" I quipped, only slightly breathy.

"I'd welcome *many* more love taps," he replied quickly, tilting his head as he watched me, like a cat playing with a mouse. "But are you brave enough to hit me again?"

I quirked an eyebrow, hiding the rush of prickles to my face with a flat-eyed stare. "You forget that I live with you, Lazarus. I could attack you anywhere, any time. Maybe I'll get you the next time you make your cat's dinner. Maybe it'll be when you're getting your coat from the closet."

"I hope it's when I'm in the shower," he countered with a shameless grin.

Ugh, beating him at anything—sparring or wordplay— was impossible.

"If you want to risk your manhood..." I shrugged. "It can be arranged. How would you prefer it harmed? By a kick or a knife?"

He didn't even wince; his eyes darkened further and he stepped into my personal space, making my breath catch. "A punch would be ideal. More personal, more intimate."

"Hacksaw it is," I said, swallowing hard.

His presence was heady, his attention even more so, and my head was foggy with it, with all of him. I couldn't think of anything he stood to gain from playing with me like this; I was already forced to help him find Lorn. Was he trying to seduce me simply because ... he wanted to?

"You're so cruel for one so lovely," he murmured, lifting his hand as if he would touch my face but leaving it hovering above my cheek. A tingling sense of anticipation rushed to my skin, and my stomach fluttered. "I should be lucky you're my ally and not an enemy."

"How do you know I'm not both?" I asked, unable to look him dead in the eye. I knew he'd see every bit of dark-edged desire I felt if I did, and I didn't know what he'd do.

I had to be smart, had to keep him at a distance so he didn't find out about Keaton being my sire. But it was difficult with him hovering over me, all sensual danger and tempting darkness. I'd never been attracted to bad guys before, preferring the reliable security of ordinary lovers, but I couldn't deny the primal tug towards Lazarus. After what happened to me in the library, after Lorn throwing me across the archives and leaving me to die, after transitioning alone, screaming through gritted teeth as the pain became unbearable ... after *that*, being close to someone deadly like Lazarus was appealing.

Anyone would have to go through him to hurt me again.

"We can spar again tomorrow night," he offered in that soft, silken voice, oblivious to the inner workings of my mind. "But fear not—I'll be on my guard for sneak attacks from fearsome librarians all through the day."

I snorted, not a particularly sexy noise but one that made Lazarus's dimple deepen. I was about to dismiss his 'fearsome' comment, but maybe he was right. Maybe I *was* kinda scary now. I liked that idea, and liked the idea of sparring just as much. Maybe I didn't need Lazarus to scare away any attackers; maybe I could do it myself, like I'd scared Thatcher tonight.

"I want you to teach me how to fight properly," I said, surprising him if the flare of his red eyes was any indication. "Not just with speed and vampire strength. I want to know how to punch, how to stop a hit like you did tonight."

Lazarus nodded, giving me that impressed, pleased look again. "Then tomorrow I'll start teaching you. But now, I'm going to go watch All Of Us Are Dead with Keith."

I froze at the soft touch he traced down my neck, so disorienting and intense that I almost overlooked the bizarreness of his daytime plans. So that was what he did instead of sleeping. Lazarus was an enigma.

He moved away, heading for the door, but I blurted, "Wait! Do you..." Self-consciousness hit for no good reason when he looked back at me. "Do you have any books? I read when I get bored."

The smile Lazarus gave me in reply was so bright it rivalled the moon.

"Come with me," he said, and vanished out the door.

With a little frown, I followed.

EIGHTEEN

I STARED, OPEN MOUTHED, AT THE TWO-STOREY LIBRARY in front of me. It was safe to say Lazarus definitely had books. Thousands upon thousands of them, all neatly shelved upon gleaming walnut bookcases. This room was more glamorous than the ballroom I'd spotted while snooping. There were gilt touches everywhere; on the mouldings framing the walls, on the sky at sunrise painted on the ceiling, on the chesterfield chairs at the far end of the room by a massive, ornate marble fireplace, and even on the plaques on each bookshelf denoting which genre it belonged to.

"I'll leave you to it," Lazarus said with a laugh at my stunned stare, and closed the door behind himself, leaving me in heaven.

"I might marry him," I told the room.

I was like Belle in the Beast's library, awed and reverent. I didn't know where to begin first, but one thing was for sure: I needed a pot of tea while I curled up in one of the chairs with a new book.

My breathing came even faster than it had while fighting Keaton earlier, an excited tremor moving through my hands. All the anxiety I'd been carrying melted away, replaced by childlike wonder.

"I love you," I told the library, staring at the mezzanine level with its intricate gold railings, marble columns, and marble busts of famous authors and poets—I spotted Elizabeth Barrett Browning, Shakespeare, Jane Austen, Rudyard Kipling, and Emily Dickinson.

"I'll be right back."

I ducked out, making a mental map of how to find the treasure trove again while I raced to the kitchen. I'd never made tea so fast in my life, tapping my fingers on the counter so fast they blurred, impatient to get back to the library and explore its offering of books. Maybe I'd even find something I'd never read before, something only a vampire might have in their collection.

"Finally," I huffed when the water began bubbling, rapidly approaching a boil, my body buzzing with excitement—or maybe adrenaline from fighting Lazarus and actually getting a hit in.

If I hadn't had vampire hearing, I'd never have heard the shatter of glass over the raucous bubbling of the water. I spun to the window and screeched as the curtain flapped up, casting a beam of sunlight on my stomach. I was covered by the fabric of my shirt, but it felt like a thousand bee stings all at once, and I shot across the kitchen at triple speed with a whimper in my throat.

The library and my tea forgotten, I cast frantically around for what had broken the window, for what had parted the curtain enough to let the dawn's light fall on me. I shook all over, adrenaline drenching my blood. I'd nearly been burned to death; as it was my stomach was seared with stabbing pain. I daren't look at the damage beneath my shirt.

What breath I had stuttered out of my lungs when I

spotted a solid glass bottle rolling across the checkerboard tiles, a flaming cloth stuffed into it. Oh gods. Holy' merciful gods. I shook even harder, my fangs chattering.

"Lazarus," I rasped, panicking. *"Lazarus!"* I cried louder, praying he'd hear me even across the house, even though my voice broke.

I gave the Molotov cocktail a very wide berth as I tiptoed around the marble island, not breathing at all as I grabbed a copper pot with shaky hands. I twisted the tap on, jumping at the sudden spray of water into the pot.

It's just water—just water. Breathe, Karina.

My stomach burned like crazy and I bit my lip, enduring the pain as I held the pot under the water, the hollow clang as it filled scraping my nerves to shreds.

Someone had thrown a bottle through the window. Someone was trying to burn the kitchen, maybe even burn the whole house down.

I shook so hard that water rushed over the edges of the pot when I picked it up, only my vampire strength making it possible to carry it. I shut out my stabbing pain as I moved around the island, as close as I dared to the flaming rag. Absolutely terrified and so conscious of how easily I could go up in flames, I emptied the vat of water on the fire.

The blazing rag sputtered but didn't go out, and I knew the fuel in the bottle would keep it stubbornly burning.

"Karina, *move,*" Lazarus said in a lethal voice, deep and furious.

I jumped, water sloshing down my front, but I instinctively scrambled away as Lazarus stalked into the room looking ready to murder someone. In my panic, I thought he was angry at me, and my stomach cramped with dread and fear.

Lazarus furiously assessed the situation, his cold gaze

sliding over me. "Fill that again. Good thinking."

With hands shaking like crazy, I did as he said, dumping more water on the fire as Lazarus soaked a towel and smothered the spitting flames with it. I was painfully aware of where the sun's pale ray fell across the room, and I made sure to stay well away.

"Careful," Lazarus warned in a terrifying voice. "Fire is fatal to vampires. We're more flammable than even humans."

My throat bobbed with a dry swallow, and I stared at him, my body equal parts weak and numb. I could have *died*. One false move, and I'd have been nothing but ash. The shadowhounds wouldn't need to use their ruthless magic to snuff me out; I'd already be dust and shadows.

I backed up until my spine met the cold brick wall, trembling so hard my hands refused to stay at my sides. I didn't want to die. I became very suddenly aware of my mortality. I might have been immortal, unable to age, but I was clearly able to die, and death hung above me like a guillotine's blade.

"There," Lazarus said, still in that deadly tone. "It's out."

But I stared at the tiles it had already blackened, stared at the fire mark that had marred the marble worktop. "Someone tried to—to—"

"It's my fault," Lazarus said, coming around the marble island, to lay a hand on my shoulder. The weight of it made my breath hitch, a strange comfort making my body cave in. "I miscalculated how Lorn would respond."

Lorn's face crossed my mind and stayed there at the forefront, tormenting me with his friendly smile and warm eyes—and then with his cruel smirk and clear evil.

I went cold all over, the burn on my stomach deeper, sharper.

"Was he trying to kill me?" I asked, my voice hoarse. I lifted my gaze to Lazarus. "Because I was supposed to die in the library? Is that why?"

I wanted him to say no, of course not, but he sighed, his violence dissolving.

"I don't know." His hand drifted from my shoulder to my cheek, and my eyes burned at the touch. "He could just as easily be trying to kill me, or to send a warning. Don't worry too much."

I choked on a laugh. He really didn't know me at all if he thought I wouldn't worry about it, if he believed I could brush these fears off my shoulder like a bit of stray lint.

"I worry about everything," I laughed. There was nothing remotely like humour in the sound.

"I'm calling in a favour from a friend," he told me, stepping away. Cold rushed in in his absence, and I wrapped my arms around myself so I wouldn't pull him back, hugging my throbbing stomach. "He'll guard the house and make sure no one else gets close."

But the damage was done to my peace of mind; the house no longer felt safe.

If we didn't find Lorn and hand him in to the council, the hounds would be sent after me. Not to mention he'd keep attacking people, risking exposing all supernaturals and bringing about the literal end of our world. No way would humans let us coexist peacefully—it would be war, gruesome and irreparable. Doomsday, through and through.

If becoming a vampire had thrown my world into panicked chaos, how would I feel if the whole world changed?

We had to find him and stop him—but now the shadowhounds weren't the only ones who'd kill me. Lorn would, too.

NINETEEN

I SAT IN THE LEATHER SEAT BY THE UNLIT FIREPLACE IN the library with a cold mug of tea in my hands, my sun-scorched stomach healing thanks to the salve Lazarus had distractedly given me. I was too shaky and numb to drink, so the cup remained full.

Lazarus sat opposite me, glaring into the dark fireplace and digging his fingernails into the chair of the arm, clearly ranting angrily inside his head. I was glad he wasn't speaking his furious thoughts; my nerves were shaky and frayed enough. I would have honestly been scared of him if he wasn't quiet right now.

I vaulted out of my seat when a door slammed near the front of the house. Lazarus shot to his feet with a hiss, crimson eyes blazing, but he relaxed when a male voice called, "Rus? It's us!"

"Us," Lazarus muttered, dragging a hand down his hair in clear agitation. Then he raised his voice and shouted, "Library!"

"Your friend?" I asked, jitters moving through my body. I

was right on the verge of running in response to my flight instincts.

"My friends," he corrected with a deep huff, returning to his seat and motioning for me to do the same.

I remained standing. Just because Lazarus wanted me alive didn't mean his friends would. My whole body clenched, ready for a fight, and I flexed my hands in case I needed to defend myself. Lazarus noted it but didn't say anything—at least not until the library door squeaked open and a tall, muscular man with a quiff of brown hair strode in.

"It's bloody freezing in here," he remarked.

"I told you to come alone, Isaiah," Lazarus replied with heavy disapproval.

"And we did," the stranger replied wryly, orange-brown eyes flicking from Lazarus to me with obvious interest.

Mortal—he was alive, with blood thrumming through his veins and life giving his olive skin a healthy flush. The small, graceful woman who followed him into the library was alive, too, a flush of exertion high on her pronounced cheeks. They were both very, very lucky I was too sick to eat right now. I shot Lazarus a mutinous look; he could have warned me.

"Isaiah, Quinn, meet Karina. She's helping me with something council-related. Karina, meet my best friends, Isaiah and Quinn."

Isaiah offered an awkward wave, obviously not sure how to treat me. That made two of us—they were Lazarus's friends, and here to help after someone threw a flaming bottle through the kitchen window, but was I supposed to treat them like I treated Lazarus? Or ignore them entirely?

"If she tries to bite me, I'll skewer her," Quinn warned in a hard voice, stalking across the rug like a precise, deadly storm. She moved with a confidence and dangerousness that I instantly envied, her heart-shaped face both beautiful and thunderous. She wore only black, from her heavy boots to her ribbed leather pants to her tight vest and jacket, making her colouring even icier. I had no idea what species she was. Fae? Elf? Angel?

Isaiah was easier to identify; when he stepped closer, eyeing me curiously, my skin crackled and buzzed with magic. He was a mage for sure. But light or dark? Did his magic do good or harm?

"She's not going to bite you," Lazarus said, rolling his eyes and seeming less inclined to trash the library just to vent his anger with his friends here. "*Are* you, Karina?"

I shook my head, retreating into myself surrounded by such big personalities. I wanted to be sharp and snarky and make an impression on them, but I couldn't find my voice. I sat, shaky and nervous.

"So what happened?" Isaiah asked, stuffing his hands in the pocket of his wool coat as he faced Lazarus.

Quinn crossed the rug to smack his arm, her expression somehow even darker, even fiercer. "I told you not to keep it from him. Stop stalling with questions, Sai."

Isaiah winced, leaning against a solid bookcase with his arms crossed and a wince on his face. "Another victim turned up, drained the same way as the others."

"Where?" Lazarus demanded, making me jump when he shot to his feet.

I wanted the chair to swallow me. I'd never felt more out of place in my life. I didn't belong here, in this circle of friends, in this stranger's house.

"Deptford," Quinn told him, her voice sharp and stripped of any attempt to sugar-coat the truth. I admired her even as she scared me. "They were found about twenty minutes before you phoned us."

"Before I phoned Sai," Lazarus pointed out with dry amusement. But his expression fell to grim resignation when he sighed. "So not only did Lorn threaten us, but he's taken more power."

"Us," Isaiah echoed with a knowing smirk. Whatever he thought he knew, he was *way* off. I doubted he'd believe Lazarus had kidnapped, imprisoned, and then strong-armed me into a bargain to help him find his progeny.

"He's taken more power," I repeated, drawing all their attention.

I swallowed and looked at Lazarus, the newness of the others making the back of my neck burn. At least I knew what to expect from Lazarus. "What do you mean power? I thought their *blood* was drained."

Blood drained, but victims left alive. That was why the Shadow Order were so adamant it was a non-vampire crime; any vampire would drain them *to death*. If Lorn was the attacker like Lazarus believed, why leave them alive?

"Rus," Quinn warned, her shocking violet eyes narrowed with reproach.

Isaiah snorted. "She's helping him with a council matter. Right?" he asked me.

I was so stunned to be directly addressed that I replied, "Yeah."

Isaiah gave Quinn a pointed look.

She rolled her eyes. "Fine. Tell the stranger we definitely can't trust all our damn secrets."

"They're not our secrets," Lazarus put in, his gaze drifting to me. I half expected to see a mirror of Quinn's distrust and suspicion on his face, but instead he just gave me a long look. Measuring whether I could handle it?

"All the victims have been from a species with magic. Angels, fae, witches, shifters, necromancers. As long as they don't die, when a vampire feeds on a species like that, we get a buzz of power from their blood."

"That's why they were left alive," I murmured, processing it. If they'd died, that buzz would die with it.

How had no one on the council connected those dots? Or had they, and chose to keep it secret? The vampire representatives must have hushed up that little fact—and then sent Lazarus to stop Lorn before he could hurt anyone else.

Which hadn't worked, clearly. How much trouble would Lazarus be in with the council now? They might have been his peers, but that didn't mean he wouldn't be punished. Or stripped of his seat.

I swallowed hard, staring at a spot on the rug as my mind raced.

"Why am I dead?" I lifted my gaze to Lazarus and repeated, "Why am I *dead*? Shouldn't he have drained me and left me in a coma like all the others?"

Anger pumped through me in the place of blood—my own blood at least. I didn't exactly *want* to be in a coma, but it made no sense. I had magic, I was a seer—I fit the profile. Why hadn't he taken magic from my blood?

"What?" Quinn demanded, her voice like a blade cleaving the atmosphere. "What the hell's she talking about, Rus?"

Isaiah crossed the rug before Lazarus could respond, drawing everyone's attention with his low murmur of realisation. My stomach twisted when he knelt in front of my chair, peering into my face. Power spat around him, invisible but potent.

"I see," Isaiah said quietly, holding me captive with the

intensity of his brown stare. I tried to move, to recoil from the magic I now saw swirling in his pupils, but I found my body locked. Trapped.

"See what?" Quinn demanded, stalking forward. Her hand flicked, and suddenly there was a small knife between her fingers, the edge flashing silver.

"Quinn," Lazarus said—one word. She rolled her eyes and halted before she could stab me, but she didn't put away her knife. "Don't be a mysterious bastard, Isaiah. And let her go, she's not our enemy. She's as much as a victim as the others."

My breath hitched to hear it out loud—I *was* a victim. I had to swallow a sudden lump in my throat at the validation.

Isaiah glanced away, and I regained control over my body, finding every part of me trembling. He was definitely a dark mage. No light mage could take over someone's body like that.

"Lorn was the one who turned her," Lazarus said, a dark edge of anger to his voice.

Isaiah flicked a glance my way, fast but significant enough to tell me he knew the real truth. But that was all he did—that single look. He didn't correct Lazarus or tell Quinn she was right to be suspicious.

I see, he'd said, and he clearly did. Did he know why I was keeping it secret? Did he know I was scared to find out what Lazarus would do if he no longer needed me?

Quinn kept hold of her knife but the look she threw at me was less murderous. "That's why she's helping you. She can use the sire bond. Huh."

She stalked over to the chair Lazarus had vacated and dropped into it, even that movement somehow threatening. Lazarus narrowed his eyes when she threw her heavy boots up on the coffee table, scattering dirt on the inlaid mother of pearl.

"I'm watching you," she warned, looking me in the eye. "One false move, and you'll find a stake buried in your heart."

"*Quinn*," Isaiah hissed, shaking his dark head. "Sorry, Karina, she's always like this."

"Stab first, ask questions later," Lazarus agreed wryly.

"I can stab you fuckers, too." Quinn scowled. "Don't think I won't."

Lazarus rolled his eyes, but he was looking at me with a contemplative look in his dark red eyes that made my stomach tighten. "You're right, Karina. It makes no sense that Lorn didn't take power from your blood, too. Unless your death was an accident."

"He threw me across a room into a solid bookcase and left me there to die. I don't think it was an accident," I fired back, my skin itching at all their attention. "He didn't care if I lived or died."

Neither of them had—not Lorn, who'd compelled me, or Keaton whose scratch had brought me back to life.

Lazarus's expression went horribly soft; I looked away, uncomfortable.

"It's a mystery," Isaiah agreed, absently twirling a spark of icy blue magic around his fingers. "What makes you different, Karina?"

I bit the inside of my lip, darting a glance at Lazarus. Was it safe to tell them about the Codex?

"Tell them anything you'd tell me," Lazarus said, glancing away when the door squeaked open and Keith trotted in, his grey tail high. "Where the *hell* have you been? I looked for you everywhere."

With an expression of raw relief on his face, Lazarus

stalked across the library and scooped the cat into his arms, pressing a long kiss to Keith's head.

I must have been staring in shock because Quinn threw her head back and laughed, and Isaiah said, "I know. The Shadow Bringer is a soft-hearted cat dad. It shocked us all when we found out."

I jolted hard, staring at the man peppering his cat with kisses. "You're the Shadow Bringer? You? You didn't think to mention that?"

He was the judge the council sent after their deadliest criminals— the ones even the shadowhounds couldn't take down. No wonder Lazarus had a row of dungeons under his house.

"Oops," Isaiah said with a cheeky grin in Lazarus's direction. Something about his expression made me think he'd let that fact slip on purpose.

"It never came up," Lazarus explained with a shrug, setting Keith down when he twisted in his arms. "Besides, you might have got scared and run."

"To where exactly?" I shot back. I had no right to be annoyed that he'd concealed that from me when I was lying about my sire. But it still rankled.

I'd been living with the council's favourite executioner all this time.

"You weren't shy to remind me I have nowhere to go unless I want to kill my entire family," I pointed out.

"Because it's *true*," Lazarus replied, throwing up his hands.

"We should have brought popcorn," Isaiah said to Quinn out of the corner of his mouth.

"I heard that!" Lazarus and I said at the same time.

Quinn snorted, using her knife to clean her fingernails.

"A vampire hearing something a mortal says? I'm flabbergasted."

I watched their interaction with interest. She wasn't afraid of him—because she was as dangerous as Lazarus, or because she trusted him? Were they friends, or lovers?

"Ha!" Isaiah laughed loudly, slanting a look in my direction. "Sorry, I just happened to be looking at you—I wasn't intentionally reading you. But no. Hell would freeze over before that happened."

My face prickled. He knew what I was thinking? Could he hear my thoughts now? What kind of dark magic did he have? I kept my gaze fixed firmly away from him, my hands curling into fists.

"What?" Lazarus asked with narrowed eyes, momentarily distracted when Keith slinked out of the shadow of a bookcase to plop himself at my feet.

The cat didn't so much as glance my way, but my heart warmed at the gesture anyway. Being killed and returning as a vampire would be a lot more bearable if I had a cat friend.

"I'm not telling you that," Isaiah replied with a low laugh. "Then *you'll* be out for my blood, too."

Lazarus made a sharp sound of surprise, and I snapped my stare up to find him looking vacantly at Isaiah. "Blood..." he murmured to himself, in his own world now.

"Any ideas?" Quinn murmured while Lazarus spaced out.

"Maybe he's hungry?" Isaiah offered, leaning against Quinn's chair to watch their friend.

My stomach churned with acid. I'd been full of dread for days; jumping to the worst conclusion now didn't take much provocation. "What is it?" I asked, biting my bottom lip.

"Blood," Lazarus replied ominously, his eyes focusing on me. "I need to check something. Be ready to leave at sunset; I'll need your sire bond."

He vanished in a blur of vampire speed, preoccupied. Leaving me with two people I didn't know, who I could easily kill if my hunger wasn't non-existent right now.

A pit of dread opened up in my gut.

He needed my sire bond—the sire bond he thought I had with Lorn.

"Better think fast, Karina," Isaiah said, but kindly.

He wasn't wrong. Unless I found a way to misdirect Lazarus, he was about to discover that I'd lied to him. And something told me he wouldn't let me sleep in his guest room and hang out with his cat when he did.

I'd be left to fend for myself.

TWENTY

Isaiah and Quinn left shortly after, to secure the house and make sure no one else would be able to attack us. I wasn't convinced I was safe here, but I *felt* it when Isaiah's shield of impenetrable magic locked around the house. A tiny knot loosened in my chest. It helped that Keith stayed at my feet, dozing with his head on his paws and the judgemental expression smoothed from his face in sleep.

I couldn't concentrate on any of the books I'd taken from the shelves, so after two wasted hours, I scrolled through old texts on my phone, relieved to see Ruby had finally answered. Her last date had been a nightmare, the guy more interested in the waitress than Ruby, but never one to let anything stop her, she'd moved on fast.

Ruby was like that—a force of nature.

I have a date with the hottest man I've seen in my entire life, her first text read, making the corners of my lips curl. She said that about all of her dates.

THE hottest man, she sent next, followed by, *and he's*

not even a Tinder hook-up, I met him in Starbucks like a real, honest to gods romance.

Twenty minutes ago, she'd sent ten pictures of herself in different dresses, along with a demanding plea that I tell her which was the sexiest one.

The strappy red one, I texted back, the normality of the moment easing the anxiety crushing my chest better than even Isaiah's magical shield. *When are you meeting him?*

Tonight, she replied instantly.

And then, *WHERE THE HELL HAVE YOU BEEN? I thought Mr Tall, Dark, and Scary had kidnapped you. I was one hour away from phoning the cops.*

I laughed out loud at how close she came to the truth, startling Keith awake. The plump feline shot to his feet and gave me a baleful glare before stalking away, vanishing into the library's darkness. There was something strangely intelligent about Keith, like a very exasperated human trapped inside a cat.

Not kidnapped, I reassured Ruby, biting my lip at the lie. If she thought I was having a thing with Lazarus, that was better than her knowing the truth. I didn't know how I'd ever tell Ruby I was a vampire.

I'd figure that out later, when I could be around her without Lazarus as chaperone.

So how big's his cock? she texted a millisecond later.

I groaned, the tips of my ears tingling. It was impossible for my mind not to instantly go down that dark, sexy path of fantasy and imagination.

I don't know yet, I replied after a too-long pause, my whole face burning. *We're taking it slow.*

Smart, Ruby praised. *Swallow too much, too soon and you could choke.*

RUBY!!! I messaged, groaning and hiding behind my hand. No one could see me here, and Lazarus was *never* going to see my texts, but I couldn't help being mortified. Curious and shivery, but mortified.

I did *not* need the image Ruby put in my head. But there was no chance I could shift it now it was there. I bit my lip, my imagination conjuring all sorts of images.

A door slammed deeper in the house and I jumped, my heart leaping into my throat.

Gotta go, I told Ruby, just in case Lazarus came back to the library. The last thing I needed was for him to find me flustered and turned on. *Text me if you need rescuing from your date.*

Vampire or not, I'd find a way to save my friend.

I rested my head against the leather chair back and gazed at the library's rows of bookcases, wanting back the untainted excitement I'd had to explore it earlier.

The attack had marred everything, until my emotions were frantic and dark. Lorn must have known I'd survived him throwing me across the archive; he must have known I'd been reborn as a vampire. Which meant Keaton knew, too.

My arms throbbed with the memory of him pressing bruises into them as he crowded me against a bookshelf, demanding I give him the codex. My arm stung with a scratch that had healed, barely a thin white line left to show there'd been an injury at all. Keaton was clearly Lorn's henchman, but he was terrifying in his own right, and I went cold all over at the thought of him.

Would he come to find me—his progeny?

I tried reading again, but it was hopeless, so after a while I retreated to my new bedroom, still feeling like an interloper as I climbed into a bed that didn't belong to me and pulled up covers that weren't really mine.

I slept fitfully, the river of blood dragging me into its depths, and I knew that whatever happened when I woke would be even worse than choking on blood.

TWENTY-ONE

I shot out of bed and halfway across the room when a fist hammered on my bedroom door, loud enough to wake the dead—pun intended. My eyes were crusted with sleep, my throat sore, and my mood about as sour as it ever got.

"What?" I demanded, wrenching the door open and scowling at the tall, annoyingly handsome vampire on the other side. "What do you want, Lazarus?"

He raised an eyebrow, his eyes trailing from the pillow creases surely in my cheeks to my rumpled clothes to my fingers, curling into fists. "It's past sunset. I told you to be ready."

I made a disgruntled sound in the back of my throat, my mood darkening at the patronising way he looked at me— like I was a cute kitten.

"I'm supposed to just do everything you tell me?" I bit out, crossing my arms over my chest and glowering at his face. "You haven't even told me what we're doing, or why. All you said was *blood*, and then gave me an order. Well, I'm not your soldier, and you don't get to command me."

I knew I'd said the wrong thing when his eyelids lowered to half-mast, an indolent smirk curling his mouth. "I think you'd enjoy my commands, baby vamp."

"Call me that one more time, and I'll stab you some-where sensitive," I warned, irritable enough to actually go through with it. Any awareness of his power and danger didn't penetrate my stormy mood, my self-preservation instincts soundly silenced.

Lazarus laughed dangerously. It only made my blood spark hotter.

"I think you might be inclined to do something other than stab me there. Unless," he purred, moving so suddenly closer that his hand was on my waist before I could blink, "it's *me* doing the stabbing."

I snorted.

"Sorry, is that supposed to be sexy? You *stabbing* me—that's the best you can do? Sounds like you could use some practise, Rus," I taunted, emphasising the name his friends called him. "Sex is supposed to feel good, not like bleeding out from a fatal wound."

Red eyes darkened, fixed on me, but he didn't budge even when I shoved at him. "Why is you saying that so attractive?"

"What?" I gave him a flat glare. "That you need practise, or 'arterial wound?'"

"Both," he groaned, his hand flexing on my waist. "I think I like the idea of you covered in blood."

I watched his throat bob with a swallow, my own tongue tingling at the mention of blood even if my dream rose all around me with its terrifying river trying to drag me under.

"In your dreams, old man," I muttered, taking a firm step back even though my legs were jelly. It was getting harder to deny the magnetic pull between us, and the fact that Lazarus was so clearly powerless to its force made it worse.

A rusty laugh burst from him, followed by a louder, warmer sound. "Ouch. I'm not that old; there are thousand-year-old vampires, you know?"

I shrugged, my arms crossed over my chest. "If you're calling me baby vamp, I'm calling you old man. Or moth-eaten bastard. Or dusty antique. Take your pick."

"Old man is fine," he huffed, smiling in a way that lit his eyes bright crimson. "Get changed," he added. "Something dark preferably. I'll wait in the kitchen."

"Where are we going?" I asked.

"Out," he answered, turning. He was gone before I could blink.

I gnashed my teeth, determined to learn that power move myself. I resigned myself to being kept in the dark as I stalked to the wardrobe and began searching the clothes hung within it.

TWENTY-TWO

I WAS GLAD TO BE OUT IN THE BLUSTERY AIR, EVEN IF the temperature wasn't biting enough to my vampire skin. I needed something to clear my head. Determined to seduce me, Lazarus had dumped a pile of weapons on the kitchen counter, and when I'd pointed out I had no idea how to strap a sheath or harness to myself, he'd proceeded to arm me in the slowest, most excruciating manner possible.

Now, I was conscious of the added weight of every slim dagger and long knife. The added bulk of the straps around my thighs and waist was unwieldy and strange, a constant reminder of who'd placed them on my body. The wooden stake sheathed at my thigh didn't weigh nearly as much as the steel, but it felt heavier.

"Stop looking at it," Lazarus chided. "It's not going to kill you."

"It could," I argued, giving him a disbelieving look as we walked along a dark path. "I'm a vampire; it's a stake."

"And it's a lot harder to find someone's heart with the end of it than you'd think. It's just for precautions, and because the sight of it will make anyone we meet think twice."

"So we're going to meet vampires?" I asked, ferreting out what information I could from the reticent vampire.

"With any luck," Lazarus replied, leading me down the river in the opposite direction to last night's journey. "Thatcher mentioned the blood moon, and Lorn becoming surprisingly powerful."

"Okay..."

"You're a seer, surely you can connect the dots. You must know magic, and how it works."

I gave him a sceptical look, holding my breath as a mortal couple passed, speaking only when they were a good distance away.

"You do know seers aren't witches, right? I don't have magic like you're thinking—smoke and spells and fire and conjuring. I just see things. But I can guess where you're going," I added begrudgingly. "You think Lorn did a ritual at the moon."

"I do," he confirmed, foreboding menace in his voice. "I think he summoned a demon, and has lost control of it."

I startled, throwing him a wide-eyed stare as cold sluiced through me. "You mean a demon's loose in London?"

I cast a fraught stare around us, scanning the buildings to our left and the river to our right, my panic escalating when Lazarus led us away from the water and into a warren of dark, moonlit streets.

"Why were you killed? That's what you asked," he said, voice low and growling. "It's been bugging me for hours, because you're right, you should be alive and catatonic in a hospital."

I shuddered, and touched the hilt of the dagger at my thigh, surprised by the solid reassurance it offered. I didn't know how to use it, but my vampire grace would lend some assistance, and I felt calmer knowing I could sink the sharp edge into anything that threatened me.

Even if that something might have been a fucking *demon*.

"The answer's obvious," Lazarus pointed out, lamplight shining on his dark hair as he guided us out to a main road full of shop fronts and slow-chugging traffic.

The noises battered my ear drums, and I flinched, my fangs bared as the cacophony threatened to overwhelm my sensitivity.

"When you think about it, the only thing that makes sense is there are two creatures to blame. One draining power from supernaturals, and one who killed you."

I ground my teeth, my ears assaulted by screeching noise and a dozen different smells stuffing up my nose before I could cut off my air—petrol puddling on the dark road, donner meat cooking in a nearby take-away, perfume and sweat, tears and blood.

People did this to themselves voluntarily—*begged* to be transformed by the Shadow Order, or surrendered to their undead lovers, or even offered themselves to sketchy vampires in night clubs. I didn't know why anyone would do this on purpose; it was unbearable.

"Don't you agree?" Lazarus asked, casting a look my way —and hissing a curse at the grimace on my face. "What's wrong?"

"Everything," I snapped, baring my fangs and wishing I could block off my hearing like I could shut down my breathing.

"Loud," I managed to hiss, barely able to hear my own voice over the honking of a bus horn and the screech of an electric scooter weaving around traffic.

Lazarus's eyes sharpened with understanding, and his arm wrapped around my back, the weight and press of it another prickling layer of sensitivity that threatened to make me explode.

He led me away from the busy road, down an alleyway between a cobblers shut for the night and a garishly bright supermarket.

I stiffened when I saw that the alley dead-ended with a trio of industrial bins and a pile of wooden pallets.

Without a word, Lazarus picked me up by my waist and sat me on the pallets, digging out a wire-wrapped phone from his pocket and ignoring my threatening snarl to put two earbuds in my ears.

I jumped when Muse's Starlight blasted, scrambling my brain for a second. Slowly orienting myself, I narrowed my eyes at Lazarus as he let go and put a few inches of space between us.

"The fuck are you playing at?" I growled, but I dug my fingernails into the wood beneath me and let the music wash over me, blocking out the other sounds.

"Trust me," he mouthed—or said. It was hard to tell with how loud the song was.

"In your dreams," I muttered, dragging air into my lungs with him between me and the humans—oblivious to the vampires just a few metres away. He'd catch me if my instincts made me snap.

I could hear myself think now, at least, with music drowning out all the other competing noises. My skin stopped prickling like ants were crawling up and down my arms. Having a single sound to overwhelm my senses was apparently a lot easier to handle than having twenty.

"Here," Lazarus said, and pulled a fucking blood bag from the inside pocket of his coat.

I stared at it, and then at his coat, and then at him. "You just carry those things around?" I asked, my voice swallowed by the roar of guitars and drums.

I had no idea what he replied—I wasn't the best at lip reading—but the insistent way he held it out spoke for itself. It was for me, then. I gave him an exasperated look, even as my mouth watered.

"You'll feel better," he said, audible in the gap between songs.

I made a scornful sound and grabbed the pouch, not allowing myself to hesitate before biting into the plastic and draining every drop of blood.

Lazarus nodded, satisfied, and motioned for me to stand while he put away the empty pouch.

Wary of getting overwhelmed by sounds again—not to mention what we'd find at our destination—I slipped one earbud out and asked, "Where's the ritual site, exactly?"

Lazarus huffed a dark laugh, his red eyes crinkled. "The ritual *site?* Karina, there are sixty, and that's just in London."

I blinked. That many ritual sites? In *London?*

"You can't expect us to check every single one," I said dubiously.

But it was clear by the amusement on his sharp-planed face that yes, he did expect that.

"We'd better get going," he said with a smirk. "We've got a long night ahead."

I stuffed the other earbud back into my ear and jumped off the wooden pallets with a groan, the stake slapping my thigh.

TWENTY-THREE

I was sick to death of charred sigils and burned grass, and especially sick of the eerie silence that hung around every ritual site. Whether it was a blackened circle in an alleyway in Lambeth or scorched grass on Clapham Common, every site was freakishly still, as if even the wind was afraid of what power clung to each scrawl and symbol.

There was dark magic, and then there was *this* magic that had been used to carve brute power from the earth. It stank of blood, brimstone, and poison, and my sensitive vampire nose burned by the end of the night.

For the twentieth time, I wondered why Lazarus had brought me with him instead of Isaiah. At least his friend had an idea of the inner workings of a spell; my seer power was all intuitive. I didn't draw sigils and chant incantations to draw fire and smoke from the ground.

"Nothing," Lazarus hissed at the twenty-third site, not too far from Fleet Street.

Traffic never really stopped in London, but on the quiet street where we stood, normality and humanity felt very far away. Looking at the magic circle sketched on the side of a bank with spray paint, anyone would think it was graffiti. I would have thought the same if Lazarus hadn't pointed it out.

I gave him a sceptical look, one earbud still in my ear, now quietly rumbling a Shinedown song and helping me focus on our task. "You're a vampire; how do you know so much about magic?"

The grin he flashed was a little too sharp, a little too fast. "There's a lot you don't know about me," he teased.

"I'm well aware of that," I shot back, not teasing.

He was far too desperate to find Lorn, refused to explain why he wanted him captured so badly, and now there was this wealth of knowledge of magic. I didn't like how little I knew about him, and how reliant I was on him.

I could maybe have tracked down Keaton myself, and used him to find Lorn, but how would I subdue a vampire much older than myself? How would I haul him to the council building? No, I needed Lazarus.

The reticent vampire didn't reply to me, instead hovering his pale hand over the wall, as if he could sense the dark magic impregnated in the stone. He didn't explain how he knew this wasn't the site we were looking for, like he hadn't at the last twenty three. He'd said the exact same thing at the others—'Nothing.'

"For all I know, this could be the site we're looking for," I pointed out, my arms crossed over my chest as I watched him in the moonlight, grim and dangerous and bristling with agitation. "We should get a witch's help."

"If a demon had come through here, you'd be able to feel it in your bones. Even other Shadow Order denizens can't stand the oppressiveness in the air. Or the stink."

"*This* circle stinks," I pointed out, wrinkling my nose.

Lazarus's low laugh ground my nerves to shreds.

"Imagine this, but ten times worse. So strong it smells like the air is a river of vomit and rotten eggs."

I gagged, taking a step back from the spray-painted sigils on the wall.

"Exactly," Lazarus agreed, seemingly unaffected by the stench. "No way has a demon come through here."

"You still don't know that's what happened to Lorn, though," I pointed out, casting a glance down the short street, wary of passersby. "He might have got power another way."

Lazarus shook his dark head. "When I saw him last, he was obsessed with demons. He—"

Lazarus cut off at the scrape of footsteps at the end of the road, and I startled, cutting off my breathing in an instant.

"Behind me," Lazarus commanded in a terrifying voice —as cold and ruthless as stone.

I hesitated for a split second, and fingers closed around my wrist like a band of iron, wrenching me behind Lazarus as he faced the five people strolling towards us—two men and two women.

My skin prickled with recognition, a strange feeling in my chest, and I stiffened when I realised they were vampires.

It couldn't be a coincidence that they'd stumbled upon us. Not the same day someone had thrown a Molotov cocktail through Lazarus's kitchen window.

"Whatever foolish plan you've cooked up," Lazarus greeted in that chilling voice, "I suggest you abandon it. This is your only warning."

A chill tripped down my spine and my fingers twitched as adrenaline flooded my system in a deluge. I took the earphone out of my ear and crammed it in my pocket with

Lazarus's phone, subtly drawing the stake from its holster at my hip. On second thoughts, I slid a dagger into my left hand, too. If Lazarus said a stake might deter someone, steel couldn't hurt either.

It became startlingly clear that while Lazarus had his secrets and I disapproved, I did trust him, at least a little.

"Lorn sends his regards," the biggest, bulkiest male said, a mean smile on his face and his hair shorn close to his skull. Like all the others, he wore full black. Like Lazarus and I did, too. Was this the unofficial vampire uniform?

"Could you *be* any more cliché?" I hissed under my breath, my nerves getting the better of me.

One of the women with the bulky vampire snorted. "She's not wrong, Wyatt."

"Shut your fucking face, Lutza," the vampire beefcake snapped.

I blinked and Lazarus was gone, racing down the road like a sharp wind. In a millisecond, he had Wyatt against the wall, his head making a sickening crunching sound. I held my breath, frozen stiff as Lazarus's brutal hand moved to the vampire's throat and crushed it with very little effort.

He stepped back and let Wyatt drop to the dirty ground, the stranger clutching at his throat, struggling for air. Vampires didn't need to breathe, but animal panic was clearly winning over logic. I knew the feeling; instinct told me to turn and run while Lazarus was distracted.

"Thanks," Lutza said, flicking her fall of golden blonde hair over her shoulder and smirking at Lazarus. "He's been a pain in my ass for weeks. You hear that?" She made a dramatic show of listening, and then sighed deeply. "Silence. Sheer bliss."

The other woman took one look at the dangerous glint in her red eyes and bolted.

"I'll be sure to tell Lorn how cowardly you turned out to be," she called in a sing-song voice. "Enjoy whatever time you have left on earth."

"You're his second," Lazarus said, watching her like a hawk with prey. I could only see his profile from where I'd frozen, but it was fearsome. "I knew Keaton couldn't be."

"That pathetic waste of air?" Lutza said with scorn, her eyes drifting from Lazarus to me. "He couldn't be a second to a squirrel."

Second? I didn't dare ask what the hell that meant. I needed to be that badass bitch who'd threatened Thatcher in an alley beside a pub, but if I was any literary heroine right now, I was Desdemona, about to die a tragic death for a bullshit reason.

I shouldn't even *be* here. That thought echoed in my ears like a heartbeat, drowning out whatever Lutza said to Lazarus next.

They were circling each other, unsure of the others' abilities. Unluckily for me, they'd forgotten about the second man.

I inhaled sharply at the sight of him stalking towards me, breath filling my lungs with the taste of dirt, sweat, and fresh bread from a bakery two streets away. I could smell blood from where Lazarus had slammed Wyatt's head into the wall, and my mouth pooled with saliva. Could vampires drink the blood of other vampires? If I lived through this, I'd ask Lazarus.

The third man didn't issue cliché warnings like Wyatt had, and didn't flee like the second woman. He blurred silently down the road and slammed into me, hard enough to send me crashing to the floor. The stake was knocked from my hand as I hit unyielding brick, but I managed to keep hold of the knife through sheer luck.

Rain soaked into my clothes from the wet ground, but it was the impact that rattled me. It made me fatally slow as the black-haired vampire grabbed my stake and threw himself upon me. Was this karma for the way I'd threatened Thatcher? I couldn't help but feel my position had been reversed.

I didn't know much about self-defence, but I knew any man's weakness. As my attacker thrust his arm through the air, stake aimed at my heart, I rammed my knee up with as much strength as I could muster—significantly more than when I'd been alive. The connection rattled up my thigh, and I gritted my teeth against the spike of pain, just managing to knock the sharp end of the stake away from my body.

"Why are you doing this?" I demanded when he fell back, clutching his crown jewels.

I scrambled back, climbing to my feet as all my senses sharpened on the hissing vampire glaring at me.

"Because you're a pain in Lorn's ass," he spat, his eyes so dark they were almost black. His nostrils flared as he got to his feet, and I was immensely relieved that a knee to the balls was a universally acknowledged pain in all species.

"*I'm* being a pain?" I laughed breathlessly, the world turning crystal clear around me as he got to his feet.

Whatever vampire instincts I had, I was glad to finally feel them instead of shivery fear. I was a predator; I had to keep reminding myself that. I might have felt like the same old Karina, but I wasn't. I was something new. Something worse. Something better?

"You're attacking me because I exist," I pointed out, stepping backward to match his step forward. He was much taller than me, but not massively bulky. Still, with vampire strength in play, lack of muscle meant nothing. *"You're* being a pain in *my* ass."

"I'm attacking you because you're supposed to be dead, and my sire is pissed off that you aren't."

Oh gods, here was someone who could expose the fact that Lorn wasn't my sire. I prayed Lazarus was too busy with Lutza to hear anything this bastard said.

"So sorry to be a nuisance," I replied, heavy on sarcasm, bracing myself when he tensed.

I dragged air into my lungs when he rushed at me, and jumped out of the way a scant *moment* before he would have slammed the stake into my stomach. My boots slid on the wet ground, but I used the momentum to carry me further from my attacker, slashing out warningly with my knife. It might not have been a stake, but nobody liked to be stabbed.

"You *should* be sorry. Actually, you should be glad it's me putting you down and not Lorn. He's not very nice to his—"

Yeah, yeah, evil monologue. I got the idea.

I threw myself forward as fast as I could, air whipping past me in a whisper and my feet blurring on the wet ground.

I told myself I was dangerous, deadly, a vampire—not a scared librarian ten miles out of her depth. I could become someone else. Right now, I needed to be a complete badass. I needed to be Xena, Warrior Princess.

The vampire lunged aside, but not fast enough to evade the sharp edge of my knife. Stabbing people was so much easier in books; when I read, the knife would plunge easily into a bad guy. There was nothing easy about this, the resistance of his clothes and skin pressing against the blade, fighting it until I threw more weight against the blow and it broke through his skin all at once.

My breathing came fast, my skin tingling all over as hairs rose up and down my arms. I'd just stabbed someone. Actually, really *stabbed* someone.

Panicking when he hissed viciously, fangs bared, I let go of the knife and stumbled back.

An abrupt scream split the air, and I flinched into the wall, my eyes wide and breathing out of my control. I forgot I didn't even *need* to breathe. Motion drew my eye as pale gold blurred a few metres away, and Lutza was suddenly on the floor. I waited for her to get back up and attack Lazarus again, but she stayed down.

I should have realised the soft huff of laughter came from my attacker, but my head was spinning.

Rough fingers closed around my throat, and I stopped breathing. My frantic stare snapped to the cold, dark eyes of the black-haired vampire as he tightened his hand around my throat, angling the stake up against my ribs. I felt it press against my shirt, cursing my coat buttons for not staying fastened while I fought.

I slammed my hand into his shoulder, into his arm, into whatever I could reach as he dug the point deeper. Once it broke skin, that would be the end of me.

I fought harder, shaking too hard to get a good hit in, and shouted in raw shock when his hand dropped, the stake clattering to the floor at my feet.

I didn't understand what had happened for the longest second, shaking hard enough that my teeth rattled. When the vampire dropped to the hard ground, the sound of his body meeting stone sickening, my breathing returned with a ragged rush.

Lazarus stood a step behind where my attacker had

been, a blood-covered spinal cord in his hand. I took one look at it and twisted away, vomiting up blood.

From the corner of my eye, I saw him drop the vampire's spine and pull a handkerchief from his pocket, cleaning the blood and fluids from his fingers.

"You're okay," he said soothingly when I straightened, shaking so hard everything blurred.

I jumped when warmth met my front and an arm wrapped around my waist.

"You're fine," he assured me, as if he hadn't just ripped out someone's *spine*. I'd known he was dangerous, but I hadn't quite realised he was a psychopath.

It shouldn't have been comforting when his hand curved around the back of my head, holding me to his chest, but I slumped into him with a shaky breath. I was alive—I was alright.

"I want to go home," I said in a small voice, wanting Mum and Aunt Jubilee more than anything. I'd even choke down disgusting-smelling casserole if it meant being near them.

"Would you settle for coming back to *my* home?" he asked—so gently that I hardly recognised his voice. "I'll even make Keith play nice and sit with you."

I huffed a hollow laugh, shock making everything numb inside me. I'd almost died, and then I'd watched a man be murdered right in front of me. He lay on the wet ground a few feet away, a gaping hole in his back.

"Karina?" Lazarus prompted, still strangely gentle.

I lifted my head and nodded. "Okay. Let's go."

This attack had made one thing very clear: I was in danger, and I had enemies following me. I couldn't go home, no matter how badly I wanted to, or the danger would follow me to my family.

TWENTY-FOUR

I TRIED NOT TO STARE AS KEITH NOISILY TUCKED INTO another home-cooked meal, but envy must have shone on my face. I missed eating, missed real food instead of blood, and the cat's gourmet dinner only reminded me that I'd never enjoy food ever again. I'd sent pictures of the dish to my family, keeping up the guise that I was at a fancy hotel for a conference. It sucked.

Lazarus sighed deeply, absently handing me a glass of rosé wine before pulling out the cloth dangling from his belt.

"Look at the mess you've made," he chided Keith when the cat turned his back on the now-empty food bowl.

With the air of a beleaguered parent, Lazarus knelt on the checkerboard floor and wiped the gravy from Keith's mouth, ignoring the daggers his beloved cat sent his way.

I felt the first smile tug my lips since I'd stabbed someone and then watched his spine get ripped out before my eyes. It should have made me fear Lazarus, but all it did was make me glad he was on my side. Maybe when the numbness wore off, fear would hit, but right now I was glad to have him in the house with me.

"Keith, have a drink," the terrifying, spine-shredding vampire instructed his cat. "Keith!" he repeated, sharper when Keith sidled past him and towards the door. "Drink! Water! I give up," he sighed when his cat disappeared from view.

"You're very strange," I told him, sipping my wine and waiting for my emotions to snap back into place. "How many people did you kill today?"

"Two. The meathead's still alive. I think." He shrugged, running a hand over his black hair—long and unbound tonight—and not looking bothered by the uncertainty of his death toll. "Let's go to the library. Sai and Quinn might have patched up the window, but I'd rather not stay in the kitchen for long."

My eyes couldn't help but drift to the ragged hole in the window above the sink. "It was definitely Lorn who threw it through the window, then."

"Him or his associates," Lazarus agreed, ushering me into the hall and down the carpeted runway towards the library.

"Minions," I corrected. "Associates implies they're equal. If they were equal, we'd have seen Lorn by now. Instead, he's hiding and letting *them* do the work."

"That's what worries me," Lazarus murmured, glancing pensively into his wine glass as he led the way down the next corridor. "Like Thatcher said, he's busy planning something."

"With the demon you think he summoned," I added, not letting myself think about *that* for too long.

There were different levels of demons—the common kind, who were drawn to hubs of human sin like pubs, sex clubs, and betting shops. They fed on their darkness, and encouraged yet more sin with whatever power they had. Generally harmless, they rarely hurt someone.

Then there were greater demons, whose power and cruelty could twist human—and some supernatural—minds to unspeakable violence. Assault and murder were their most common crimes, but if a demon managed to corrupt enough humans at once, they could do enough damage to wipe out a city.

The worst demons, so terrifying that even greater demons preferred not to speak of them, were the princes of hell. A prince's power was endless, their hunger just as vast.

And now I belonged to the same order as them. My stomach twisted, threatening to evict my wine.

"Come," Lazarus said, holding the library door open for me—and Keith who showed up out of nowhere. It was such a sudden appearance that I—a damn vampire—jumped.

I gave the cat a narrowed, suspicious glance. Where had he come from? Was he ... magic?

No, that was nonsense. He was just a sneaky cat.

"You can tell me about working in the Witching Library," Lazarus said warmly, closing the door behind us. "I've always wondered what that place's secrets are."

"The secrets are on full display," I replied dryly, sinking into a leather armchair by the unlit fireplace and making a sound of surprise when Keith jumped onto my lap. "You just have to know where to look. Hello."

Keith blinked at me, and without ceremony began to knead my stomach with his paws, sharp claws poking free but never scratching my soft blue jumper. I'd changed out of my dirty, bloody clothes, dressing in jeans, a vest, and the jumper whose owner I had no idea of. Lazarus hadn't been forthcoming.

"Smart kitty," Lazarus said proudly, sitting opposite me and stretching out his long legs on the rug, looking both tired and relaxed. "I didn't even have to bribe him to befriend you. He can sense your distress."

I held myself carefully still as Keith turned around three times and then plopped down on my lap, a warm, vibrating puddle of fur. Tentatively, I brushed a finger down his back, some of the numbness thawing from my chest when his purr deepened.

"How are you feeling?" Lazarus asked, as if he'd been waiting to ask for a while.

I debated lying, but he'd already seen me weak once tonight so what was the point of covering up more weakness?

"I'm not," I replied, stroking Keith. "Feeling, I mean."

A deep V formed between his brows. "That's not good for a vampire, Karina."

I shrugged. I wasn't doing it on purpose. "I'll be fine. I'm just not used to violence like that."

Lazarus leaned forward in the padded leather chair, his eyes measuring. "Seeing violence, or perpetrating it?"

My mouth thinned. "I didn't need the reminder, thanks."

He dragged a hand through his hair, distracting me for a second with the cavalier fall of black strands over his forehead.

"No matter how hard I hoped, I didn't think we'd find anything tonight. I certainly didn't think we'd be attacked. Still, I should have prepared you better."

I shrugged, stroking Keith, and sipped what was left of my wine.

"Let's practise again, I can teach you moves to defend yourself."

"Some other time," I replied flatly. "I'd like to stay here."

He nodded, and got out of his chair without another word, leaving me to my numbness—or so I thought until he returned a minute later with a thick, fleece blanket in his hands. I didn't move a single inch, frozen in surprise as he laid it over my shoulders and tucked in the ends around Keith.

"You can't feel the heat," he explained, leaning over me to give his cat a scratch behind the ears, "but the weight might help. Sleep if you can. I'll stay here if you're scared of another attack. I've been meaning to get through this anyway," he added, and reached for a romance paperback on a nearby table.

I blinked, surprised anew by Lazarus's contradictions. He was an ancient vampire the council sent after their deadliest criminals, and he was a cat dad who read romance books, and he tore spines out of his enemies.

To save me—he'd torn out that spine to save me.

"Why did you do it?" I asked, realising it had been bothering me. "Why did you save me? You could find Lorn without me; the sire bond hasn't been much help so far. I couldn't sense anything at any of the ritual sites."

Obviously not from Lorn, but not from Keaton either. I'd be able to sense if *he'd* been near, at least according to Lazarus.

Lazarus looked at me for so long that I became uncomfortable. "I could tell you I'm not a heinous person, that I try not to kill unless necessary, and I'm a councilmember, so letting a fledgling die on my watch would be both embarrassing and problematic."

"You *could* tell me that?" I asked, frowning.

Lazarus shrugged, leaning back in his chair, and looking at Keith curled up in my lap.

"Something about you interests me. And more than that, you're overwhelmed, out of your depth, and fumbling through your second life. You deserve a chance to live it for longer than a few days. It would be a shame to lose you."

I blinked. *It would be a shame to lose you.*

"Thanks," I murmured. What else did you say when someone said something like that?

"Get some sleep," Lazarus replied, cracking open his book and looking absurdly casual.

"Here?" I demanded, but I was uninclined to move Keith now he was breathing deeply, a heavy lump on my lap. "With you watching me?" I scoffed.

"I'm reading," he pointed out without looking up, paper rustling as he turned the page.

"Suit yourself," he said after a while. "But you'll be safer here with me than on your own."

"I thought Isaiah had shielded the house," I said uneasily, fighting the heavy tug of my eyelids. If someone could get to us here ... would they do worse than a Molotov cocktail next time? "Why are you so worried if he's made the house safe?"

"I'd rather not take the risk," Lazarus replied calmly, glancing at me above his book before he turned another page. "Am I so horrible that you don't want to be in the same room as me?"

I made a sound in the back of my throat. "You know you're not."

"Still." The edge of his mouth flicked up. "I could stand to hear your opinion."

I rolled my eyes, not about to inflate his ego. "You're fine."

"A lofty compliment," he drawled.

"Don't let it go to your head," I fired back, but a yawn

stretched my mouth. I knew I was exhausted, but I didn't trust Lazarus enough to sleep in the same room as him. He could do anything.

And yet, he'd saved my life tonight. I sighed, not sure what the hell to think about that. And when it had come down to it, when we were under attack I *had* trusted him. I was just lying to myself.

Feelings were creeping back into my chest—fear and dread and a niggling sense of doom. But none of them centred around Lazarus attacking me in my sleep. Only him kicking me out when he found out I'd lied.

Rain pelted the windows, but the heavy curtains muffled the sound to an ambient murmur, and my eyelids slid heavy over my eyes. The odd rustle of Lazarus turning pages and the rumble of Keith's purr only coaxed me deeper to sleep, no matter how hard I fought to stay awake.

TWENTY-FIVE

THE LAST THING I WANTED TO DO THE NEXT NIGHT WAS go back out into the city and resume our search for the ritual site Lorn *might* have used to bring a demon into London. I never asked Lazarus what kind of demon he believed his progeny had raised, but it was obvious he wasn't doing all this for a lesser demon.

"Here," Lazarus said, stalking into the sitting room where I waited among Chintz furniture and outdated wallpaper, the wall opposite me covered in photo frames full of portraits. I didn't recognise any of the faces except Lazarus's, which often appeared with a dignified, silver-haired woman who reminded me of Cate Blanchett.

I turned away from the photos, and when I realised what he was holding out to me—and what it meant for me in this new body—I jumped several steps across the rug.

"Have you lost your damn mind?"

"It's properly sealed," he assured me, his red eyes patient and understanding. I wasn't sure if the sympathetic side I kept seeing in him made me like him more or made him get on my nerves more. I might have been deserving of pity after being killed and reborn, but I didn't want it, dammit. I just wanted to get on with this life now, figure out a way to bring Lorn to the council, master my hunger, and go the fuck home.

"I'm not taking that from you," I said firmly, my eyes glued to the wooden ampoule in his hand, the stopper hinged with shining brass and a matching brass cross decorating the curve of the body. Holy water—he wanted me to carry fucking *holy water*. I might have been a rookie vampire, but even I knew it was deadly for us.

"I'd feel safer if you carried it," he said, watching me glower at the wooden vial.

"*You'd* feel safer?" I demanded, snapping my stare up to his deep red eyes. "Why do you care what happens to me?"

"I'd love to know the answer to that, too," he replied dryly. "Just take it, Karina. It's sealed tight; it won't hurt you."

"Unless I accidentally *open* the seal," I muttered, but I was so surprised when he caught my hand in his warm, dry fingers, that I let him put the ampoule in my palm.

"Fine," I sighed. "For your peace of mind, I'll carry this water that could, and probably *will*, kill me."

"It won't kill you," he teased, dropping a disarming kiss on the top of my head before he stepped back and assembled his own arsenal. "It'll burn your legs off, worst case scenario."

"Oh, well good job I don't *need* my legs," I huffed caustically. "Oh, wait."

He snorted. "Better that than Lorn getting hold of you."

"Why would Lorn want anything to do with me? I'm just someone he turned and left for dead." It was so close to the truth that my voice twisted into something bitter.

"You're clever and resilient. He could make use of

someone like you, and not for anything good," Lazarus explained ominously.

I got distracted as he strapped knives and stakes on his waist and arms, sheathing a broadsword across his back that he hadn't worn yesterday. I gulped as he placed three vials of holy water in a belt slung around his black jeans, tucking something I couldn't identify into the inner pocket of his leather jacket.

I let his words echo through me, and imagined all the ways a powerful vampire could use a fledgling who didn't know how to fight back.

"We should have sparred today," I said uneasily.

"You needed to rest," Lazarus replied, waving a pale hand. "Violence takes a toll, especially on the mind, which exhausts the body. We'll train tomorrow."

I'd hold him to that promise. I needed to know how to defend myself, and even one lesson would be an advantage in my current state.

"Do you think we'll find an active site?"

One that had been used recently, and for more than a luck ritual or to gain social media followers—something Lazarus said happened alarmingly often. He'd finally explained why he'd dismissed the sites yesterday, even if he didn't tell me how he could sense magic at all.

"If we don't, it's back to square one," Lazarus muttered. "But if I'm right, we'll find evidence of a demon at one of the sites. And you'll be able to sense Lorn's signature."

I frowned until he explained, "All vampires have one. You're probably familiar with mine, whether you realise it or not. You'd be able to sense me in a location I'd visited, even if I'd left days ago."

And anyone who'd met me—i.e. Lazarus—would be

able to find me, too. It was a good job I trusted him not to kill me now.

"Anything else I need to know about being a vampire?" I asked, my voice barbed. "Anything else you've kept from me?"

"Kept from you?" He raised an eyebrow, eyes glinting wryly. "There's a library full of books, many of them written by vampires *about* vampires. Moreover, anything you want to know, you may ask me, and I'll answer to the best of my ability. I've kept nothing from you."

I ignored the prickling in my face—part embarrassment, part nonsensical arousal at his use of the word *moreover*. I'd always found intelligence sexy, and there was no doubt that Lazarus was highly intellectual. Why couldn't he have been an uneducated asshole vampire? I'd be so much less distracted.

Thankfully, Lazarus wasn't aware of my internal battle. He gathered up a bandolier of knives and a mess of straps I knew went held knives around a thigh.

I held painfully still—vampire still—as he buckled them on my body, every graze and brush of his fingers sending shocks through my jeans and black T-shirt into the skin tingling beneath.

I had a feeling he enjoyed my reaction, something smug about the set of his mouth.

"You're ready," he pronounced, setting the ampoule of holy water in a secure pouch on my belt. "Just let me go say goodbye to Keith, and we can go. Here's your jacket."

I gratefully pulled on the black leather, hiding the goosebumps on my arms, and hoped tonight would be much, *much* less eventful than last night.

But even with half a dozen more weapons on my body

than before, I couldn't help feeling like a lamb walking to the slaughter.

TWENTY-SIX

Mʏ ꜱᴛᴏᴍᴀᴄʜ ᴛɪɢʜᴛᴇɴᴇᴅ ʟɪᴋᴇ ꜱᴏᴍᴇᴏɴᴇ ʜᴀᴅ ᴄʟᴀᴍᴘᴇᴅ a vice around it as we neared the tenth ritual site of the night, and a rush of stabbing warmth—somewhere between painful and pleasant—moved down my spine and up my arms.

Lazarus's head snapped around at whatever sound I'd made. We were on the edge of a charred circle in Holland Park, the ritual marks invisible until we'd passed a demarcation line. No human would have crossed it, or even known it was there; even for Lazarus and me, it had been a battle to pass through the dark power.

Now we were inside the shield, my ears popped and I shuddered at the hot prickles moving across my skin.

"He was here," I said through gritted teeth.

If Keaton had been here, Lorn certainly had. And I didn't need Lazarus to explain why this site was different from the others.

The scent of brimstone cloyed the air with rotting drains, fish, and eggs, and the sigil circle was different to the others, more complex with a hundred tiny symbols clustered and overlapping until my eyes hurt to look at it.

Not to mention a dozen pints of blood splashed the ground, still fresh even though the blood moon was two weeks ago. The shield spell must have kept the site fresh.

I wrinkled my nose, my senses overwhelmed with coppery blood and burning brimstone even *with* my breathing cut off. I swore I could hear a whistling scream, almost like the circle kept an open doorway between here and hell.

"I need to phone the council," Lazarus said in his scary, flat tone. A shiver went down my spine at the look in his eyes—there was nothing human there, nothing even remotely resembling the man who'd cooked dinner for Keith and joked with me about being a cat butler this evening. "Wait here. Don't touch the circle."

I shot him an alarmed stare. "Why the hell would I?"

Lazarus didn't reply, just grabbed his phone and stalked to the edge of the invisible demarcation line. I was painfully aware of the deadly power thumping from the circle of sigils, and I backed up a step, waiting for some denizen of hell to leap through it and tackle me.

I didn't breathe the whole time Lazarus spoke to the council in a low tone, barely keeping a reign on his anger when they replied something he wasn't happy with.

"This is *proof*," he growled in a voice I'd never heard before. I clutched the edges of my jacket, memorising where my knives and stakes were. Not that I expected Lazarus to take his anger out on me, but I barely knew him. It didn't hurt to be prepared, as Ruby would say. "It's proof that he was here, he's summoned a demon, and probably made a damn *bargain* with it!"

I pricked my ears, but the reply from the other end was beyond my hearing.

"Admit I've found more than you expected me to," Lazarus hissed, his voice as chilly as the wind that sliced through my leather jacket. "I'll find Lorn, I just need more time than the end of the damn month. You set me up to lose."

I'd never heard Lazarus say any of this, and I suddenly understood why he'd kidnapped me, brought me into his home, trusted me around Keith and his friends, and strong-armed me into helping him. He was desperate. Not just because it was his job, but because he was working without the council's help.

You set me up to lose. Did the council not want him to find Lorn? Did they want the vampire loose around London, draining power from more and more supernaturals? Or did they just not care either way if we were exposed to humans?

There were some supernaturals, especially in the Shadow and Beast Orders, who wanted to come out of the darkness and rule over mortals.

"Come on, Victoire," Lazarus hissed. I pricked my ears, committing that name to memory. "You *know* Lorn needs to be stopped. You're playing with fire. Here's proof of what he's done, and what even worse deeds he could commit. Give me a task force. Stop fucking sabotaging me."

I just barely picked up a feminine laugh, like the high, haunting sound of a ringing glass.

"Victoire, my seat's at fucking risk—"

He snarled, throaty and guttural, and I flinched, turning sideways so I could see both the deadly circle and the dangerous vampire throwing his phone to the ground.

I watched, not breathing, as he stalked to a tree and

threw a punch so hard it splintered the trunk, and then another, and another, until branches broke and fell down around him.

"Lazarus," I whispered, not wanting his wrath to swing to me, but alarmed by the blood I smelled—fresh, *his*.

He spun, fangs bared, with a guttural threat in the back of his throat. I stumbled away on instinct, a chill crawling up the back of my throat, intensifying the prickling heat down my spine.

"Stop!" he shouted, deep with compulsion and rage.

My foot froze mid-air, my whole body locking.

I swore tendrils of magic rippled from his shoulders as he sped across the park to me, blurring between one spot and the next, but when he grabbed me and dragged me into him, nothing but leather clung to his body.

And I realised I'd been mere inches from the charred circle. Close enough to topple in.

Oh holy fuck. What would have happened if I'd stepped into it? Would it have sucked me into hell?

Still shaking with rage, still hissing, Lazarus set me down a safe distance from the smouldering circle of runes, and lashed out at another tree, kicking the ground with a destructive hit that had dirt and grass spraying up around him.

"Why is this so important to you?" I asked breathlessly, allowing a scrap of air into my lungs. My head spun, probably why I thought it was a good idea to question a vampire in the middle of a destructive rage. "Finding Lorn, impressing the council—why is it so important?"

It felt personal, and not just because Lorn was his creation.

Lazarus spun, his pale face gaunt and covered in dark,

scrolling veins, his eyes so red they were almost black, deadly fangs bared on a throaty warning.

I froze, wanting to take a step back but afraid to go near the circle again.

"I need my seat on the council," he replied gutturally, danger hanging around him, making my skin buzz with warning. "I don't owe you a damn explanation, Karina."

I shook my head, irritation thawing some of my terror. "How am I supposed to trust you when you won't tell me why you want Lorn so badly?"

I blinked, my words echoing in my own ears. "Are you and he—?"

Lazarus was in front of me in a rush of air and menace. "Not that I have to explain myself to *you*," he sneered, "but no. Now mind your own damn business, Karina."

My breath caught when he stalked away, his back a tight line under his coat and his hands vibrating with rage at his sides.

"You can't just leave me here!" I protested, outrage thumping in my chest in the absence of a heartbeat. "What about the circle?"

Lazarus didn't turn back, didn't even reply. I hurried after him, but between one heartbeat and the next he was gone.

"Fine," I ground out, gnashing my fangs. "Go sulk, that's fine by me."

I had a vague idea of how to get back to his house; I could find my way there. But did I really *want* to return to a house with someone I knew was keeping something big from me, who wouldn't even hint at his motives?

Maybe he was testing me by leaving me here. Maybe he wanted to see if I'd go on a murder spree. I tried to ignore the way my fangs throbbed at the idea of blood, turning to look at the charred circle in the grass instead.

Maybe Lazarus had just stalked off in a toddler-esque tantrum. I didn't know what Victoire had told him across the phone, but she clearly wasn't pleased by the discovery of this circle. She wanted Lorn, and Lorn alone. At least I knew the council's motives—avoiding supernatural exposure. But what the hell did Lazarus get out of it beyond keeping his seat?

I shook my head, my jaw set, and gave one last look to the faintly smoking circle before I set off walking, the demarcation line's magic shivering over my arms as I crossed it. I'd decide whether I was going back to Lazarus's house later; now I just needed to get moving before the sun decided to rise, or I'd be toast. Probably literally.

If I'd been more daring, more like the characters in my favourite books, I'd have gone off to find Lorn myself. I'd drag him to the council and use him to buy my own innocence, or at least some help in navigating vampire life.

Maybe I should have gone to a vampire House; someone there would help, right?

The only issue was I had no idea where any House was. Only vampires did, and apparently rebirth didn't come with that secret knowledge unlocked in my brain.

Plus, going after Lorn by myself seemed like a recipe for true, final death. I'd nearly been killed by one of his minions; I had to assume I had no choice against the vampire Thatcher called super-powered.

My phone buzzed in the pocket of my dark jeans. Relieved to have a distraction as I left the park—and the circle—behind, I fished it out, a weight falling off my shoulders when I saw Ruby had texted. This was what I needed

—to talk to my best friend and forget about everything else for a little while.

I laughed when I saw she'd sent a video. My guess was it was a dozen different outfit options, from slinky dresses to hot blouses and curve-hugging jeans. A smile curled my lips as I waited for it to load—and then my breath cut out and I froze in the middle of the path, my whole body shocked cold.

Ruby was there, but she wasn't smiling or twirling in a pretty dress. She was beaten and bruised, tied to a chair with rope and silver chains.

I didn't notice the background, didn't see the man standing behind the chair for a long moment, fixated on my unconscious best friend as blood clotted her hair.

"You should be dead," the pleasant voice I remembered from the library remarked, and I jumped, my eyes shooting to the attractive, blonde man resting his hands on Lex's chair and smiling at the camera. "But I'll happily take your pretty friend's life instead. If you'd prefer to offer yourself in her stead, you have one hour."

TWENTY-SEVEN

I WAS SO STUNNED AND TERRIFIED THAT I DIDN'T HEAR
the address and had to hit replay, my eyes blurring with
blood tears as I watched Ruby slumped in the chair, very
faintly breathing but not otherwise moving.

With shaking fingers, I typed the address into Google
Maps and wiped blood from my eyes with the back of my
hand.

The image of Ruby unconscious and bloody was
burned on my retinas, a swollen lump stuck in the back of
my throat as I hurried in the direction of the address.

Wasn't it enough that I'd died because of Lorn and
Keaton? Now my best friend's life was in danger.

If you'd prefer to offer yourself in her stead…

Cold gripped my whole body despite the warmth of the
air against my skin. I didn't want to die. I wanted to live, to
go home and see my mum and aunt, to slot back into my old
life and figure out a way to hide that I was dead.

I didn't want to die again. The first time had been
endless and painful and petrifying. I knew there'd be no
coming back from whatever death Lorn would deal me.

Where the hell had Lazarus stormed off to? I should never have let him leave, should have screamed and yelled until he came back.

I didn't have his number, didn't have any way of contacting him besides phoning the Shadow Council's helpline—but judging by unhelpful Victoire, if I called them, things could go from bad to worse. Phoning human police was out of the equation with vampires in the mix, and the supernatural force wouldn't get involved in council business.

I was on my own.

Helpless rage rushed through me as I sprinted around a corner, following the map's arrow. A noxious mix of emotions bubbled in me, and I slammed my fist into the side of the café I'd just passed, wincing at the crack of pain through my knuckles and up my wrist.

A spiderweb of cracks formed in the plaster under my fist and guilt twisted my stomach as I backed away, fleeing the scene of the crime. Once I started running, I couldn't stop, breath sawing out of my lungs and my legs like jelly. Only my superior eyesight kept the map's arrow steady in my vision as my hand jerked wildly.

London blurred past, and I didn't care enough to check my speed as I raced past mortals and supernaturals alike, a streak of panic and red hair. The closer the little arrow on my phone got to the pin of my destination, the more sick I felt.

I verged deeper into the city, the sky lightening from star-studded pitch to deep navy to purple. I realised where I was being led when tall, golden spires came into view, capped with pure white domes. This was an angel temple. What the hell was a vampire doing here?

I slowed, my breathing frantic, at the end of the road.

How many vampires would be here? At least Lorn, and probably Keaton. I took a ragged breath and felt for that prickling warmth I'd felt back at the ritual site in Holland Park. A slight tingle crawled down the back of my neck; I had to assume that meant my sire was here. But how many others?

It didn't matter; I couldn't *let* it matter. Ruby was in here, and it was all my fault. No heroine in any book I'd read had shrugged and gone home when their bestie was in danger, and I wasn't about to either.

So even though my hands shook, I drew a knife and a stake. I cut off my breathing so I couldn't smell Ruby's blood as I crept closer to the temple, the columns out front elaborately carved with wings and feathers, halos, and swords. I hadn't known which angel this was a temple to, but judging by the scenes of both beauty and violence, it was an avenging angel. Great.

Maybe I should have called for help after all. It would have been nice for someone to know where I was, even if it was an uncaring council member.

It was reckless, but I texted Mum and Aunt Jubilee before I ascended the ornate golden steps. Two words: love you. At least if I didn't get out of here alive—well, still undead—I'd told them that much.

It felt like I'd been on borrowed time since I slammed into that bookcase in the Witching Library anyway.

Gripping my stake and knife hard enough to snap them in two, I took the steps up to the angel temple where a vampire madman waited.

TWENTY-EIGHT

INSIDE THE TEMPLE, SILENCE WRAPPED AROUND ME like a death shroud. It was too quiet. No screams, no hisses, not even a breath echoing nearby. All my senses heightened at the danger lurking around every ornate corner, my eyes frantically scanning carvings and frescoes and rows after rows of golden pews.

My skin stabbed with my sire's nearness.

Paranoid, I tilted my head back and scanned the rafters. Not a single shadow moved, no vampire hiding among the beams. But I *knew* I was being watched, and a shiver hovered at the top of my spine. Someone here, watching me search the pews for my friend, watching me open doors on empty rooms, braced for Lorn to jump out.

I wished Lazarus was here with a fierceness that surprised me. At least he had my back; he wouldn't have ripped out that vampire's spine if he didn't. No one was coming to save me, and unless I figured out how to give Lorn what he wanted, I couldn't save Ruby.

She didn't deserve any of this. Neither did I, but this was my dark, fucked up world now. Maybe the only way to stand a chance was to match their darkness with my own. To stop clinging to humanity, to stop pretending.

I shuddered, moving further into the temple, down a golden hallway lined with portraits of famous and influential angels—singers, actors, politicians, humanitarians, artists, writers, dancers. Even if I didn't know all their names, each face was recognisable. I hadn't realised there were so many popular angels, or that they were honoured here in a temple.

Shouldn't my blood have boiled being in such a holy place? Shouldn't my skin have crawled and burned?

"In here, Karina," Lorn's amiable voice called, and I froze between one step and the next, a chill shuddering through me.

Adrenaline kicked in, my hearing sharpening until I could pick out the barely-there sound of someone very quietly moving, and I could taste blood and sweat on the air, could sense the vibration of bodies poised to attack.

It definitely wasn't just Lorn here waiting for me.

I cursed Lazarus for not teaching me anything useful that I could use to fight, but I walked as fast as I dared down the hallway in the direction of Lorn's voice. The closer I got, the more my skin stung and stabbed.

I braced myself for the sight of Ruby, limp and bleeding and bound to a chair. I had to get her out of here. I didn't know how the hell I'd do that, but I had to.

"No need to be so afraid," Lorn said with a smile as I finally reached the open archway to the room he occupied— a circular marble room full of glass cabinets cluttered with golden astrolabes, intricate globes, bronze sculptures, and priceless vases with tiny, painted angels around the rim. "I can hear you shaking from here. Come in, and say hello to your best friend."

I froze on the edge of the room, my gaze pinned to Ruby. It took me a moment to realise there were three other people in the room—my sire, a brown-haired vampire, and a man with fire-red skin and jet black eyes in an impeccable suit, currently sharpening his long, vicious fingernails.

A demon. The demon Lorn had summoned was here.

TWENTY-NINE

Blood oozed from pustules all over the demon's skin, soaking through the expensive suit he wore. He turned toward me, rough features sharpening with interest that made my stomach twist.

"Come in, come in," Lorn coaxed, as if he didn't have my unconscious best friend tied to a chair. I prayed he'd knocked her out with compulsion and not something worse, but I didn't trust the psycho as far as I could throw him.

I took a hesitant step across the threshold, hating the way my weapons shook in my hands. The knife and stake seemed measly now, and definitely not enough to take on three vampires and a demon. Buzzing stabbed up and down my arms the closer I got to Keaton; I ignored my sire even if I could sense his eyes on me, oily and threatening.

"I'm here," I said, looking at Lorn and only Lorn. His smile softened his face into rugged handsomeness, his blond hair swept artfully around his face and the cut of his white shirt and trousers precise, expensive. Yet, with his sleeves rolled up and his hands in his pockets, he seemed casual. Relaxed.

It was all a game to him—luring me here, kidnapping Ruby. I just didn't know what role I was supposed to play.

"Let her go," I ordered, recoiling when the demon let out a soft growl, almost like a purr, and turned towards me.

The very corner of Lorn's mouth curved sharper, and he settled his hands on Ruby's shoulders. "I just need one small favour from you first, Karina."

"Let her go, and *then* I'll do your favour," I countered, too breathy, too afraid. My whole body was shaking now, the suffocating presence of the demon crushing my chest as his full focus pinned on me.

There was one thing I knew for sure—he wasn't a lesser demon.

Lorn tsked, and the door slammed with a resounding boom behind me, echoing off the curved walls and the dome above.

I flinched, spinning breathlessly. A hulking vampire vaguely reminiscent of Wyatt blocked the closed door, fangs bared as he crossed massive arms over his chest. I was trapped in a room with four vampires, a demon, and my unconscious best friend.

Still, one huge vampire was slightly better odds than three vampires and a demon. But that would mean leaving Ruby behind, and that thought made me sick.

I suddenly understood why all those literary characters were willing to gamble with their own lives but not the lives of their loved ones.

"All you need to do for me," Lorn said, watching me, "is read a page from a book. That's all."

I narrowed my eyes, instantly suspicious. It couldn't be that easy; no way.

"Why can't you read it yourself?" I asked, watching

where his fingernails dug into Ruby's shoulders, drawing pricks of blood through her glitzy sequin dress.

She'd gotten dressed up, her hair vaguely retaining a bouncy curl, and eyeshadow smeared with the blood on her swollen face.

"I'd like you to read it instead," Lorn insisted mildly. "All you need to do is put your weapons away and read from a book. Then you can go home."

I knew he was lying, but with a hulking vampire at my back and worse threats in front of me, I had to play for time.

So I nodded, putting the knife back in its sheath. I kept hold of my knife. I could hold a book one-handed after all.

Lorn appeared pleased at the compromise, a light entering his red eyes as he motioned at Keaton.

I backed up for two reasons—my sire gave me such a dark, sinister look that I knew he instantly wanted me dead, and he held the Codex of Fiends in his hands, fingertips pressed gingerly to its cover as if it would burn him.

I should have figured out what book Lorn meant. If I hadn't been so terrified, I would have put two and two together sooner.

"You could have made me read it in the library," I pointed out, giving Keaton an icy glare as fury and fear whipped into something destructive in my chest. "You had me compelled—why not do it then?"

The third, as yet silent, vampire snorted. He leant his elegant frame against a glass case full of portraits and lockets, his smirk irreverent and careless and brown hair tousled.

"Our illustrious leader thought one demon would be enough then. Now he's got a taste for power."

Lorn hissed, releasing Ruby to step threateningly towards the vampire who didn't even blink at the warning.

"What?" the brown-haired vamp shrugged, his smirk deepening. "You're gonna kill her anyway; why not tell her all your secrets? Get a load off your chest, y'know? I hear therapy's good for you."

"You're on thin fucking ice, Will Hewett," Lorn said, his upper lip curling back from sharp, elongated fangs.

Power pulsed through the air, stealing all the air from my lungs, crushing the oxygen from the blood in my veins, and my bones creaked and ached until weakness sent me to the floor.

I wasn't the only one—Keaton had dropped the Codex and bent in half, his head in his hands. Will Hewett was clearly insane; even curled up on the ground, he laughed through his screams.

I tried so hard to hold onto what Will had let slip, something about greed and demons, but my mind scrambled. The discomfort in my bones dialled up to pain, my eyeballs stabbing and tears rolling down my cheeks. This was worse than even dark magic, *so* much worse than what Isaiah had done by trapping me in his gaze. I'd never felt *anything* like this before.

"Apologise," Lorn commanded, lifting Will's head with the dagger-like tip of his shiny shoe. I half expected him to kick the silver edge into Will's throat and sever his head. Blood ran from the vampire's eyes and nose like it ran through mine, responding to Lorn's twisted power.

What the hell *was* this power? Was this what he'd made a deal with the demon for?

I gritted my teeth against a scream as the pain spiked in my bones, horrible retching sounds coming from my throat as I gasped for air I shouldn't need.

"Any more and you'll kill all of them," a deep, foreboding voice rumbled, like an avalanche of deadly, broken rocks and too-close thunder. "I'd rather you kept this one alive. It appeals to me."

I flinched as a proprietary hand slid from my neck and down the knobs of my spine.

"You can have her after," Lorn huffed, and suddenly I could breathe, could think, could feel something other than pain.

A hand lingered on my back, burning like molten earth.

I wrenched away, teeth bared in a reflexive warning, skin crawling all across my body.

The demon had touched me, and now he stood above me, watching with hunger-dark eyes.

I shuddered hard, moving blindly backwards until I slammed into a glass case, my hands shaking so violently I couldn't get them to still.

You can have her after.

After *what?* And have me *for* what? None of the options that crossed my mind were good. It said a lot about my situation that the demon wanting to eat me was probably my best case scenario.

"Useless," Lorn muttered, kicking Keaton's hand aside as he reached for the Codex of Fiends. A few yellowed pages of the ancient were strewn across the marble floor, the binding ruined by the drop. "Here, Karina. Be a good girl and take this. Read this page from top to bottom, and you can leave."

I climbed warily to my feet, not liking how everyone loomed over me, but I didn't lift my hands to accept the book.

My breath came faster, but I forced my voice to be even when I said, "He just said you're gonna kill me. Why should I give you what you want?"

If my last act was defiance, so be it. I'd much rather my last act be saving Ruby, though.

Lorn flashed sharp fangs, advancing on me and shoving the book against my chest. My fingers curled around it on instinct, another page fluttering out as it trembled in my grip. I stubbornly held onto my knife, balancing both in my grip.

"Read, or I snap your pretty friend's neck. Now!" he boomed when I hesitated.

A hint of that agonising power—demon magic and vampire dominance somehow, impossibly mingled—pressed on my shoulders, and I gasped, flattening out the page he'd opened.

Oh, gods. Oh holy fucking gods. He didn't want me to reel off a list of demon's names from the encyclopaedia; Lorn wanted me to read a ritual spell to unbind the gateways of hell.

Every ritual site Lazarus and I had visited would become a doorway between London and all hell's worst nightmares.

It was the end of the world, and I held the key to its destruction in my hands.

I suddenly understood why it was kept behind lock and key in the archives, even if I didn't understand why the book hadn't been burned centuries ago. Cold crept across my spine as the demon sidled closer, his presence impossible to miss—like ice and fire burning my skin, his scent of brimstone, guts, and rotten fish turning my stomach.

"I—I can't read this," I rasped, not daring to look at Lorn. "I can't read Abyssarian."

The slap came so suddenly that my head slammed into the glass cabinet behind me, shattering it into a thousand shards and sending pain rupturing through my skull.

Heat cracked across my face where Lorn had back-handed me. My head spun, shock making everything fuzzy for long seconds.

"I know for a fact you can, Karina Dobrev," Lorn seethed. "You're fluent in nine languages, two of which are dying demon languages, and one of which is Abyssarian. So *read*. And know that for every lie you tell me, I'll slice off one of poor Ruby's fingers."

Breath rushed out of me with a whimper. I nodded and blinked fast, focussing on the ritual spell.

There was no way out. Either I read this and unleashed hell, or he'd kill Ruby and then me. Maybe he'd kill me anyway, but at least I could stall for a little while.

With a ragged breath, I began to read.

THIRTY

THE VISION OF MY DEAD CLIENT FLASHED BEHIND MY eyes as I haltingly read the first paragraph on the yellowed page. The dense, intricate language tripped clumsily off my tongue in breathless phrases as I fixated on that memory. He'd been killed because of this book. So had I.

All because Lorn was greedy for power. This spell would unbind every gateway to hell—not just in London, I realised as I read, but all across the country. If enough power was fuelled into the spell, maybe it would reach across the world.

I didn't have my own power, not the kind of raw magic the spell needed, but Lorn who'd spent weeks sucking up his victims' magic ... he certainly had enough to bring half of hell to earth.

The council was worried humans would turn on us when they found out we lived amongst them. They should have been more worried about living in a world overrun by demons.

"Faster," the demon coaxed at my back, his heat hitting

me in waves that tightened my stomach. "My language tastes so good on your tongue."

I shuddered in revulsion, stumbling over the next phrase, scrambling for a way to change the spell, to fuck it up without any of them knowing. Would it be better to die than unbind hell?

I knew the answer, but I wasn't selfless enough to sacrifice myself. I was scared down to my bones; I wanted to *live*.

Long, razor-sharp fingernails curved over my shoulder, and my voice jumped and broke. Lorn gave the demon a throaty hiss of warning. Behind him, my sire and Will Hewett moved, but I couldn't lift my eyes from the page to see what they were doing.

How many demons would come through the unbound gateways? The biggest gates were watched over by gatekeepers, but the smaller ones like in Holland Park were vulnerable and unprotected. How many humans would be slaughtered and corrupted? How many supernaturals would join their cruelty out of fear or greed or lack of better choices?

Within weeks, an army of demons could overrun the whole country. All because I couldn't figure out another way out of this nightmare.

Something hot and wet slithered up my neck, and I screamed, dropping the Codex to the floor and skittering away.

Laughing, the demon flicked its long, forked tongue at me. My stomach roiled as I backed away, stumbling into the chair Ruby was bound to.

My breathing cut out when she cracked an eye open before closing it again. Okay. Okay, she was alright. If I untied her bindings, maybe we could fight our way out together.

A new vampire and a light witch against four vampires and a demon. Those weren't good odds. Not at fucking all. But it was better than finishing that spell.

"Get out!" Lorn growled, deep and guttural. "She'll have to start over again thanks to you and your greed."

"*My* greed?"

The demon laughed, an awful, chittering sound that chilled my blood. Its rough-hewn face crinkled with a fang-filled smile that made even Lorn reconsider his position.

I used the frozen tension to slide my knife over the ropes at Ruby's back, not daring to drop my gaze from Lorn but guiding the blade by touch.

"You, pathetic vampire, who begged me for power? Who'll beg my brethren for the same power? You, who feels so insignificant and unworthy that you're desperate for magic to assert yourself over other vampires?"

I struggled with my knife, and nicked my finger, but that didn't matter so much as the unravelling of a single thread. Hopefully it was enough for Ruby to run when there was an opening.

Another laugh from the demon, a short chuff of sound. "Yes, vampire, speak to me of greed."

Lorn said nothing in reply, but his face was as dark as night when he spun to pin me with a glare. I straightened, hoping he didn't notice the tiny slice in Ruby's bindings.

I lifted my knife in pitiful warning when he rushed across the floor in a silent blur, clawed fingers suddenly in my hair. Pain flashed across my skull when they twisted, but it didn't stop me struggling against him.

I snarled, the sound far from human, and tears of blood veiled my sight as I was dragged back to the book. Lorn shoved me to the floor in an ungracious heap. My knife tumbled out of my hands and across the floor, and I choked on a cry. I had others on my body, but drawing them would earn more of Lorn's wrath.

"*Read,*" Lorn snarled, nothing mild or friendly in his handsome face now. He couldn't take out his anger on the demon, so he'd loose it upon me.

Disoriented, I nodded my agreement, gathering the book in unsteady hands. My head throbbed where he'd pulled out hair strands, but I bit my cheek and frantically flipped pages, trying to find the right spell.

Or ... could I trick him? It was stupid, suicidal probably, but I found a page as densely packed as the first—a spell to force a demon to reveal their true name—and began to rapidly read, stumbling over words too fast for Lorn to notice they were different.

I made it through the first paragraph, and then the second, but the demon growled so deep and loud the glass cabinets exploded, raining glass around us.

I flinched, shaking as I waited to be attacked.

"Fuck!" Keaton swore, glaring daggers at the crimson demon as glass cut his face. The way he looked at the demon ... it was like he was jealous, like the hellish creature had stolen his best friend. I sneered, not recognising the feel of my lip curling, my nose wrinkling, but not caring enough to change it.

Breathless, I hurried through the next paragraph as the world shook around me and I struggled for air.

"She's reading the wrong spell," the demon roared, bursting my ear drums, and making every sound fuzzy and dull.

I read faster, digging my fingers into the pages when Lorn dragged me to my feet, spitting the last few sentences until power rang through my voice. Some rituals required innate magic, but some could be wielded by anyone.

"Invequius," the demon screamed, syllables dragged from him by a darker, older magic than anything Lorn possessed. Every species knew there was power in a name, especially fae and demons who could be controlled by their true name.

"Invequius, I bind thee," I gasped, a shout ripped from me when Lorn's eyes flashed deadly red, filling all my vision, and his hands slammed into my chest, exactly as they had in the Witching Library.

Deja vu spun around me as I flew across the room, memory merging with the present until dizziness ate every thought in my head.

I hit the solid marble wall hard enough that something snapped in my arm, and I screamed, my harrowing voice echoing over and over in my muffled hearing.

Again—he'd broken me again.

THIRTY-ONE

A LOUD, THUMP SOUNDED IN MY EARS, AND THEN another, and another, and for a delirious second I thought it was my heartbeat. But I was dead—Lorn had stopped my heart when he'd tossed me aside like rubbish to be discarded.

I ground my fangs, my vision sharpening without warning, the dizziness vanishing like a blanket ripped off my head. When I heaved myself along the floor, my hands slid through blood, and that powerful thud sounded again.

I dragged myself by my fingernails, my hearing clearing with a rough pop that brought hisses and growls of arguing vampires and a furious demon.

Right, I'd forgotten that I'd been promised to him, to do whatever he wanted. He must have been pretty pissed off that I was damaged. Maybe he didn't like his meat tenderised. And maybe I was delirious and fucked in the head for that thought.

I shook my head to clear it, flinching when air whooshed around me without warning. I snapped my head to the side, but there was no leering demon there, only ... only wings. As red as blood and as tough as leather, veined with black shadows like ink through marble.

Wings—I had fucking wings.

"Well," a dry voice remarked, "you just got far more interesting."

I snarled in warning as footsteps neared, baring sharp teeth at Will Hewett's smirking face as he crouched in front of me, reaching out to trace the velvety edge of a wing. I hissed at the shot of sensation, somewhere on the border of overwhelming pain, and wrenched away.

"That," Lorn said, thumping footsteps cracking the floor, each one a threat that wound my muscles tighter, "is highly inconvenient."

He could have blurred with vampire speed, but he wanted me scared. For that reason, I summoned a throaty hiss and struggled to get my feet under me. The weight of two leathery wings threw me off balance, but for some asinine reason, Will steadied me with a hand on my arm.

"Of course you'd inherit dearest grandmother's Bane form," Lorn said, his perfect face twisted with disgust. "This is your fault," he spat, whipping around to Keaton who hovered at the edge of the room, nursing a scowl. "If you hadn't scratched her like an imbecile, she'd have died. Or at best, she'd have stayed fucking compelled."

Keaton flinched.

I tried and failed to tuck my wings closer to my body, wobbling on my feet—easy prey for a seething vampire. What did he mean I'd inherited his grandmother's Bane form?

"*Well?*" Lorn flung his arms out at his sides, his eyes manic with rage. I noticed everyone, even the vampire doorman, kept their distance. "Apologise."

Keaton inhaled sharply, but lowered his dark head. "My gravest apologies, my sire."

Sire? I inhaled sharply, my wings twitching in response to my emotions. I almost wanted to laugh. Lazarus had spent all this time thinking Lorn was my sire, and instead he was my ... what, grandsire? No wonder I'd inherited a family trait; I *was* Lorn's family.

"Time to go," Will Hewett murmured in my ear, grazing my wing either accidentally or intentionally.

Black claws punched through my fingertips in response to the threat of his closeness, and I hissed, slashing at his face. Pale skin split against inky, vicious claws, blood bubbling on Will's cheek like rubies, but he just smirked.

I didn't know what a Bane form was, or how I had one, but if it got me out of this room, I didn't give a shit. My chances of surviving had gone from zero to one percent, and I had no intention of letting go of that tiny gleam of hope.

I tore the ampoule of holy water from the pouch on my belt and threw it with all my vampire strength at Lorn's feet. The wood shattered on contact, water drenching his legs. Just the scent of it made my tongue burn, my nose scorched.

Lorn's roar filled the room, and I dove for Ruby, praying I was fast enough to grab her and get out. The room blurred as I pushed myself faster than I'd ever moved before, air whipping past sensitive wings and making my eyes water.

My fingertips brushed the rough weave of Ruby's bindings, rope slashing under my sharp claws, and she jumped to her feet, taking a wobbly step.

Her head swivelled as she searched for me. I moved too fast for her to spot me, and I couldn't help but be glad she didn't see my wings. My Bane form.

Nothing good ever included the word *bane*, did it?

"Karina," she whispered, fear drenching my name as she

backed up, scanning the room for me.

I lunged for her arm to speed her out of the room, out of the whole damn temple, but the heavy door at the end of the room blasted open.

The menacing vampire guard stumbled forward a step as—as his body cut in two at the waist. My stomach roared with nausea as the man's torso slid gruesomely from his bottom half before both butchered parts smacked into the floor.

Ruby screamed, bursting my ear drums. I spun away on instinct, fangs gritted. I couldn't breathe, couldn't get the image of the vampire cut in half out of my head, the gore imprinted on my eyes.

Light exploded through the room while I was dazed and horrified, and it felt like the bottom fell out of my world. Sunlight—fat golden beams blasted into the room, promising to burn me to a crisp.

Please. It didn't matter which god heard me; I sent the prayer to every one of them. *Please, please...*

I spun vampire-fast, frantic for a way out, but the sunlight blocked the exit, racing closer from the open doorway as shadowed figures spilled into the room.

A body slammed into me, and all the air crushed from my lungs as a heavy weight flattened me to the floor. It happened so suddenly that dizziness didn't get a chance to form, so suddenly that my head bounced off the brutal marble floor and rebounded into a solid chest.

"Stay down," a rough voice commanded, and I began to shake.

Once my legs started quivering, so did my arms, and then my whole body. I couldn't get it to stop, trembling and out of control. My teeth clacked together. I knew that voice —Lazarus.

Thank you. The gods had heard me, had spared me.

"Oh, you think so, do you?" a dark feminine voice laughed a few paces away, followed by a vampire's guttural hiss.

Was that ... Quinn? Was Isaiah here, too?

"What's happening?" I choked out, shaking harder.

They'd come for me—or for Lorn, but the distinction didn't matter. They were *here*, and the death that had been crouched on my shoulders, scythe around my throat, had been pushed away. I could get out, I could live.

I could *live*.

"Just stay down," Lazarus bit out. "You're going to be fine, but stay down."

"Shit—Sai!" Quinn shouted, nowhere near as amused as she'd been a few seconds ago. "Don't let him grab the—"

Lazarus hissed, his frustration evident, but he didn't move from where he'd thrown himself over me—shielding me from the sun, I realised, and my bottom lip caved in. Blood tears welled in my eyes. I didn't want to break right now, but I couldn't control my reaction.

I'd nearly unleashed all hell, nearly lost my best friend, nearly been assaulted by a demon and murdered by the same vampire who'd killed me the first time.

I flinched at the sound of Lorn's voice now, oily and smug. "Let's do this again sometime," he said, as if this was afternoon tea and not a violent attack.

"Don't let him go!" Lazarus roared, making my ears ring. He shifted against my back—and then groaned in pain and flattened himself to me again.

"Shit!" a rough male voice spat. Isaiah, maybe, or Will. Where was Keaton? Where was my sire? I shook harder.

"He's gone, isn't he?" I rasped, my eyes screwed shut and the floor cold on my cheek. "Lorn got away."

THIRTY-TWO

A BREATH PUNCHED OUT OF LAZARUS, AND HIS forehead lowered to my shoulder, strands of silken hair brushing my wing. Hot, electric sensations shot through my body, confusing the hell out of my emotions.

"It certainly sounds like he's gone," he agreed.

Lorn would come back for me. I knew it. Whether he could find someone else to read from the Codex, he'd come for *me*. It was personal now—I'd pissed him off.

"Alright, the sun box's shut," Isaiah called across the room, his voice recognisable this time. "You three can get up."

Three? I frowned, but I was shaking too hard to fumble a meaning from his words.

"Ruby," I rasped. I didn't know what a sun box was, but Isaiah was on our side and I trusted him enough to take his word that we could get up.

"I'm fine," my best friend was huffing, pushing away the concerned dark mage who hovered around her, eyeing her bruises, the blood matted in her hair, and the limp she walked with. "I don't need babying; I need to see my best friend."

Oh gods, my wings, the claws, my eyes that were almost certainly deep red—

My knees shook as Lazarus climbed off me and helped me to my feet, his eyes burning as he watched me closely. I avoided his gaze, not wanting to know what he thought of this Bane form thing.

I couldn't breathe as I turned to my best friend, who didn't even know I was undead let alone whatever the hell this was.

"Ruby, I—"

She met my eyes and launched across the room, naked relief on her heart-shaped face. Lazarus stepped neatly in front of me before she could come closer than a few feet, his hand snaring in the collar of Ruby's dress.

"Let me go, dickwipe," she snarled, her voice hoarse but full of the sharpness and sass I loved. "Don't think I won't kick you in your vampire balls."

A laugh-sob lodged in my throat, and my eyes stung fiercely.

"She could hurt you," Lazarus explained, with zero patience in his voice. Losing Lorn must have felt like acid in a wound. I glanced around for the demon and my shoulders slumped when I realised Invequius had vanished, too. But he was bound to me; I knew his name. I could call him back whenever I wanted. My stomach flipped at the thought.

I glanced up as Ruby ploughed right through Lazarus, taking him off guard enough to reach me. I locked down my breathing in an instant, but I was too sick and terrified to even *think* about blood right now.

Ruby didn't spare more than a glance for the wings, the

eyes, the fangs—she wrenched me into a strangling hug and held on for long, long seconds.

"Jesus, you're freezing," she hissed.

I had no idea how to reply to that. She was shockingly warm, like plunging into a scalding bath, her arms like ropes of burning fire around my middle. I didn't know why it was so comforting, but a weight fell off my shoulders.

"I thought you were dead," she said shakily, squeezing tight enough that I choked out a sound of discomfort. "When he threw you across the room—"

"*Who?*" a deadly voice demanded, and I jumped, goosebumps skimming my arms.

"Back off," Ruby snapped. "She was my best friend before she was ever your girlfriend."

"I'm not," I protested with a sigh. "It's ... complicated," I finished, instead of saying he'd stopped me killing more people by locking me in his dungeon basement. Besides, knowing Ruby she'd think a dungeon basement was sexy.

"More complicated than the wings?" Ruby asked dryly, squeezing my middle in reassurance before I could begin to spiral.

I swallowed. "I have no idea what's happening, or what I am, or why I have these. I just—I want to get out of this place."

"What should we do with this guy, Rus?" Quinn's sharp voice cut across the room, and I glanced up to watch her grab Will's arm hard enough to bruise. "I vote cut him into lots of little pieces."

"Heartless, Quinn," Will remarked, that irreverent smirk back on his narrow face.

"I'll bury every piece under a different nunnery. Even if you come back as a ghost, the only company you'll have will be nuns."

"Seems harsh on the nuns, but okay," he chuckled.

"Knock it off, you two," Lazarus growled, deep with warning. He sounded ready to tear someone limb from limb himself. "Ruby, we'll drop you off at the hospital or your home, whichever you prefer. Karina, you're coming back with us. Will—you've got some explaining to do."

"Ugh," Will sighed, sounding like a petulant teenager as he raked a hand through his flowing brown hair. "I hate *explaining*."

"Tough shit," Lazarus fired back. "Start thinking of what you're going to say to me. If it isn't a good story, I'll have your damn fangs."

I blinked, surprised they knew each other but baffled by their dynamic.

"Is your guy like..." Ruby whispered, "his brother?"

Will barked a laugh, hearing Ruby perfectly with his advanced senses. I angled myself in front of her when his attention fixed on my best friend, shooting him a warning glare. I had a pet demon now, and I wasn't afraid to use him to protect my friend.

"He's more like my dad, sweetness," Will explained with a crooked smile.

It fell off his face when Isaiah whacked him upside the head. "Shameless flirt. The woman's traumatised; leave her alone."

"Well, let's not be too hasty," Ruby complained, shooting me a conspiratorial look that made me feel human and accepted as a vampire all at once. We needed to have a real, long conversation about me being undead, but I didn't have the energy for it yet.

I jumped as a shadow moved beside me, but it was just Lazarus looming, silently assessing me for—actually I had no clue what. I gave him a tired, exasperated glance.

"What happened?" he asked, that dark edge still clinging to his voice.

"Later," I sighed, heading for the door in the hopes everyone would follow. Lazarus caught up to me instantly, like a stalwart knight at my side.

"I'll take you to the hospital," Isaiah offered to Ruby, steadier and calmer than the smirking man at his side.

"No offence, Orange-Eyes, but you could be a psychopath for all I know. My last date didn't turn out so well," Ruby added dryly. "I'm going with Karina and Dick-wipe over there."

A laugh startled from my mouth, and I couldn't help but smile even as I glanced at Lazarus. "Can she come back with us?"

The *please* was implied.

He glanced between us, red eyes narrowed and tight, but he groaned, "*Fine*. But only for one night. And if you piss off my cat, I'm throwing you out."

Quinn rolled her eyes. "That damn cat."

"Don't insult my best friend," Will complained, the smirking vampire throwing an arm around Quinn's shoulders.

"Keith hates you," Lazarus drawled, guiding me out of the room I'd almost died in. Shattered glass lay everywhere, blood pooled on the floor. I was glad to leave it behind.

"I'll get the van," Isaiah offered, running ahead. "I probably don't have to say this, but I will anyway because I don't trust you not to be idiots. *Do not* go near the windows *or* open a door. It's full daylight outside."

I stiffened. Right. I must have been in here an hour—maybe longer.

I jumped as a hand skimmed my back, but I should have known it was Lazarus. I jumped harder when his phone blared a shrill cry that made my ears ring like earlier.

"Kaine," he bit out, an unfriendly answer.

My heart sank when he stiffened, his hand flexing on my spine.

"I see," he said coldly. There was a pocket of silence where I should have heard another voice, but instead heard nothing. "Well, I'm going to respectfully disagree. You're welcome to try the wards on my house. For now, I think you have bigger things to worry about, Victoire."

He stabbed the *end call* button and shoved the phone back in his pocket.

"The call was veiled," I breathed, nerves choking me. "What did she say?"

"Nothing you need to worry about," he assured me, guiding me down another corridor and scanning for windows.

I halted, giving Lazarus as stern a look I could summon after a nightmare like today. "Don't lie to me, Lazarus."

"Do you want me to castrate him for you?" Ruby offered seriously, watching us closely.

I shook my head, not taking my demanding stare from Lazarus.

He pressed his lips into a firm line. "The council wants you in custody. They think you're assisting Lorn, and you've unleashed a demon on London."

The warmth drained from my body, and I swallowed against a dry throat.

"I—I haven't—" But it was a weak protest when I had a demon's true name. "Lazarus—"

"It's okay," he said gently, anger blazing in his eyes but his hands gentle when he settled them on my shoulders. "They're not going to arrest you. As soon as we're home, they can't touch you. We still have two weeks before their deadline; we can find Lorn and end this."

"I can help," Will offered.

"You can stay out of it," Lazarus snapped. "You've caused enough trouble."

"Yeah? And what about the information I've gathered on Lorn and his best demon buddy?" Will Hewett laughed smugly at the look Lazarus shot his way. "Not so trouble-making now, huh?"

"You might prove useful after all, pretty boy," Quinn drawled.

Will gasped dramatically. "She thinks I'm pretty," he whispered. And then louder, "Besides, if we're talking about trouble, we should talk about the ritual they were making your girlfriend read out. I'd say it's more than enough to destabilise the gateways, even without them being fully open."

Lazarus shot me a look of pure alarm, and I shrank back, my hands shaking.

"It wasn't her fault," Ruby snapped. From the corner of my eye, I saw her shove Will into the wall, and my heart leapt into my throat. But he didn't retaliate, didn't use his advanced senses against her. He just splayed on the wall and laughed, delighted.

Ruby turned to Lazarus, giving me a worried look, too. "It wasn't her fault. He would have killed us both. And fuck knows what the demon would have done if Karina hadn't been clever enough to bind it."

My shoulders hunched; I tried to make myself smaller. She was trying to help, but this was going from bad to worse.

"Don't throw me out," I pleaded with Lazarus, not brave

enough to meet his eyes. "I'll stay in my room, I won't bother you, but please, I need somewhere to stay."

"*Karina*," he said, horrified. Great. Now I had no choice but to go home where I'd hurt my mum and aunt. Or live on the streets. Maybe I'd get lucky and one of the vampire Houses would take me in, but I knew I wouldn't last a day in one of those dens of violence and power struggles.

"Of course I'm not throwing you out," Lazarus huffed, squeezing my arm as he angled closer. "And I don't blame you for anything that happened; of course you were just trying to save yourself and your friend. But the council won't see it that way, so we need to lay low."

"You're not kicking me out," I said, frowning at him—at the anger still darkening his eyes and pressing his mouth thin. For the first time, I realised it might not be at me, but at Lorn, or maybe at himself for losing Lorn.

Footsteps hurried towards us, and I tensed, my hand fluttering to a small knife still strapped to my thigh. I sagged when Isaiah rounded the corner, his dark hair rumpled and his eyes intense. "The car's ready. Let's go."

I didn't understand how I fit into this group yet, but at least someone had my back. I glanced at Ruby, guilt at accidentally dragging her into this making me sick.

"We're gonna be fine," she promised, noticing my attention. "We survived that." She stabbed a finger in the direction of the circular room we'd just escaped. "How much worse can it get?"

With the council after me, the threat of shadowhounds hanging like a noose around my neck, Lorn on the loose, the gateways unstable between earth and hell, and a demon bound to me rampaging across London ... worse.

Much, much worse.

☾

Thank you for picking up Vampire Librarian - I hope you loved Karina and Lazarus! There's more vampires, magic, and simmering romance coming in book two, Vampire Shadow. It releases later this year.

You can let me know if you loved the book by leaving a review, and preordering Vampire Shadow. If you guys need the next book asap, I'll bump it up my schedule as much as possible!

Thanks for the support you've shown so far—it means the world to know you love Karina as much as I do <3

Kristin x

BOOK TWO: VAMPIRE SHADOW

Karina's story continues in book two of The Shadow Order:
Vampire urban fantasy series!

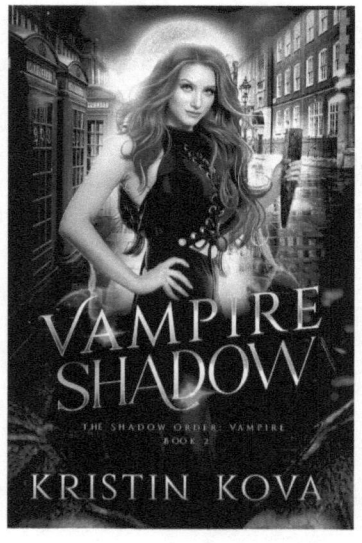

Preorder it now on all retailers!

TWO FREE URBAN FANTASY STORIES

Fancy some kickass freebies? I'll send you two when you join my newsletter! I promise never to spam you, and I rarely send more frequently than once a month so you won't be overloaded with emails.

Join here: https://sendfox.com/kristinkova

ABOUT THE AUTHOR

Wickedly Good Urban Fantasy

Kristin Kova is an urban fantasy author from the UK. She writes about regular (albeit supernatural) women who kick ass, and magic-packed stories full of heart and action with a side of sizzling steam.

The first book in her debut series, The Shadow Order: Vampire, is out now, and you can pick up two urban fantasy stories for free by joining her newsletter.

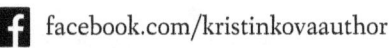 facebook.com/kristinkovaauthor

bookbub.com/authors/kristin-kova

FIND THESE OTHER BOOKS BY KRISTIN
KOVA!

The Shadow Order: Vampire

Vampire Librarian

Vampire Shadow (Late 2022)